MW01135863

SOMETHING WICKED

UNIVERSITY OF MORGANA: ACADEMY OF ENCHANTMENTS & WITCHCRAFT

EMMA DEAN

Emma Dean

SOMETHING WICKED
UNIVERSITY OF MORGANA:
ACADEMY OF ENCHANTMENTS AND WITCHCRAFT

All rights reserved. No part of this book may be used or reproduced in
any manner whatsoever without permission, except in the case of brief
quotations embodied in critical articles and reviews.

Copyright © 2019 by Emma Dean

This is a work of fiction. All of the characters, locations, organizations,
and events portrayed in this novel are either products of the imagination
or are used fictitiously. Any resemblance to actual events or locales or
persons, living or dead, is entirely coincidental.

AUTHOR'S NOTE

All of my paranormal books exist in the same universe. The more you read the more you see familiar faces. You don't need to read them in any particular order, or to know any others before starting any of my series or standalones.

This series heavily features Kenzie and her foxes from The Chaos of Foxes series, but there is nothing from that series that is needed to read this one. Everything has been explained.

Last but not least, this is a slow burn reverse harem series. Don't forget to share and review and recommend your favorite books.

And yes, there will be sexy sex in the series ;)

<3 Emma

It was night, and the rain fell; and falling, it was rain, but, having fallen, it was blood.

- Edgar Allan Poe

SOMETHING WICKED

Mika shut her last suitcase and set it on top of her trunk. She surveyed her room one last time and sighed. She wasn't going to miss this place. Not after everything that had happened last fall.

The Marshall Clan was one of the oldest witch clans in San Francisco and now all that was left of it was her grandmother, her sister, and Mika. They'd been a well-respected clan until Mackenzie Kavanagh uncovered Bradley Davis's plot to overthrow female witches in the Bay Coven and revealed her brother and father were involved.

She would never forget the feeling she'd had watching that insanity unfold.

When Bradley had called out both her father and her brother as co-conspirators to his plot...Mika had never felt so betrayed. All the air in the room had disappeared. The oxygen in her lungs had been sucked out like some kind of creature feeding off her very air. Mika had only ever experienced that level of panic—fear, once.

The heat had come first when the men in her family had been hauled to their feet. Her entire body was flooded with it and then everything went ice cold.

That was when the ringing in her ears had started. It hadn't really stopped since.

Mika couldn't remember much after that. Vaguely she recalled her mother screaming as they'd dragged her brother away. Her father though – he'd somehow walked to that line of perpetrators with grace.

There was no doubt in her mind that her father had dragged her brother Jacob down that road with him.

But they had both made their choices.

It was still hard to comprehend exactly how they could have gotten in league with that piece of trash, Bradley. It made her physically ill every time she thought about it. Most days she was okay if she was very careful not to think – not to do much more than breathe.

Then suddenly she'd remember a time Jacob had been kind to her, or her father had told her he was proud of her – then it hit her like a ton of bricks and she relived that moment in the coven building all over again.

And that always triggered the memory of what Bradley had done to her all those years ago.

Mika checked her watch to make sure she wasn't going to be late. Then she sat down on top of her trunk and looked around one last time. This would always be her room – she would come back here after she graduated and live here for the rest of her life. That was the witch way.

But that would be five years from now.

It was weird to think about.

And it didn't help that she was starting a semester late thanks to everything.

The betrayal by her father and brother hadn't been the worst of it either. The heartbreak had devastated her mother. She'd never recovered. The next heir to the Marshall Clan had wasted away until she just...no longer existed anymore.

It wasn't like her mother had simply gone to sleep and never woken up. She didn't just die one day. No, Mika had watched her break—shatter that day in the coven building, and she'd disappeared a little at a time like a leak in a dam until suddenly there was nothing left of her.

All the doctors said there was nothing that could have been done. Even the High Priestess Takahashi had come to try to talk to her mother. But nothing could shake her; nothing could heal her mother's broken heart.

Mika smoothed her hand over her skirt, eyeing the gloves she always wore out. She was almost positive her brother's betrayal had been the real cause – not her father. He had always been their mother's favorite.

Now her older sister was slated to be the new heir to the Marshall clan. She would become matriarch when their grandmother passed.

Claire was almost as powerful as Selene Kavanagh, the youngest Kavanagh matriarch in generations.

Mika remembered what it was like to go to school with Selene. The other witch had been a prodigy, and had graduated early so they'd drifted apart. But Selene had always been kind.

"Mika!" her sister called up. Claire's voice echoed in the empty mansion. "Are you ready to go? We've got to get you settled today!"

There was so much to take care of...it felt like they'd just barely gotten everything turned in after winter solstice and yule.

Starting in the spring semester...Mika wasn't looking forward to it.

Instead of responding she grabbed her things and dragged them down the stairs.

Claire grabbed the trunk from her when Mika hit the main floor. Her sister tried to smile. "Don't worry. You're going to love the university. It's like high school, but a thousand times better."

Mika gritted her teeth together and still didn't say anything.

She'd hated high school and everything about it. If Selene was a prodigy, then Mika was the most mediocre, average witch to ever attend their high school. She was the same age as Selene and lightyears behind her in magical skill.

It didn't really matter though in the long run. She'd just barely passed the entrance exams to the University of Morgana. At least she hadn't completely tarnished her family's name.

Mika had gotten a perfect score on the theory of

magic. It was so unprecedented they'd tested her again with a proctor watching every move she made.

The test had been completely different, and she'd still aced it.

But the practical? Ugh, she didn't want to think about that. Actual magic had always been *meh* for her. Lighting a candle took concentration on her part. A three-year-old could do it with barely a thought.

"The door to the university is in the coven building," Claire explained as they made their way through the foyer. "I'll go with you, but you'll have to cross on your own. Someone needs to look after Grandma until she decides to rejoin the land of the living."

"She's still alive," Mika murmured. "That's more than we can say for our parents and brother."

"That's not fair," Claire snapped, letting the driver open the front door for them. "Dad and Jacob are still alive. They're just stripped of their powers and shunned."

Mika popped open her umbrella and glared up at the never-ending rain. Where she was going would be colder, but at least it wouldn't be raining. "Dad and Jacob are dead to me after what they did to us and Mom. Let's not pretend we'd ever have them over for dinner."

Her sister didn't say anything to that, and Mika didn't expect her to.

It *wasn't* fair on Claire, but she was still so angry. Mika lived that moment over and over and had been all fall and winter. Then sitting at her mother's side for months and simply watching her waste away...

No matter how much she loved her mother, Mom

hadn't loved them enough to fight and live and…just be around. She'd given up on everything even though Mika had been *right there* every, single, day.

Claire followed after her to the fancy black car without an umbrella, letting the rain mess with her perfect hair. She let the driver take Mika's trunk from her and stood there in the rain. Mika knew in that moment she should say sorry, but she was just so angry and bitter and devastated. It would only rip her apart even more to apologize for saying what she felt.

Once everything was loaded up, Claire kissed Mika on the cheek gently and stepped back. "On second thought I should stay with Grandma. Who knows what an empty mansion will do to her. I wish you the best of luck, baby sis. Write home and all that."

Mika held her sister's gaze and it was like looking in a broken mirror. They both had the same nearly white-blonde hair that was their family signature, ice blue eyes, and skin so smooth and creamy people often stopped them and asked them what their secret was. Their next question was if they were twins.

Claire was only an inch taller than her, but she had the better tits.

"If you need anything or…" Mika trailed off. She almost couldn't say it out loud. "If anything else happens, call me. My phone is always on."

Her sister nodded and Mika got in the car. Claire didn't slam her door closed, but it was forceful just the same. Mika flinched and regretted those words she couldn't take back, even if she wanted to.

The last six months had exacerbated everything she'd been hiding for the last three years and now...

It felt like everything she'd shoved down and ignored was all frothing to the surface, ready to boil over and she couldn't pretend anymore.

Mika didn't know how to pretend to be happy, or how to be...normal.

What was normal in the witch world anyway?

Kenzie was a void witch after spending most of her life a pariah – an abomination.

And up until she'd announced it to the coven no one had even known void witches existed or what a void was exactly – a witch who didn't have powers, but could take them. Something the universe had created for balance no doubt. Mika didn't know the details of a void's skills, but knowing someone could take her magic...

Things were changing. She just had to get through this and onto the other side.

It would get better. It had to.

"Take me to the coven building, please," she asked the driver, words barely above a whisper. Speaking out loud always seemed so harsh in the sudden quiet that had befallen her family the moment her mother had fainted in that fateful meeting.

As soon as Mika got settled on campus she would call her sister and apologize. But right now she was still pissed and the only thing that would come of her calling her sister was an argument. Claire didn't deserve that – not with everything she had to deal with now.

Claire was going to be the next Marshall matriarch, and thank the Fates.

Mika didn't want it.

She didn't deserve it.

2

The door to the University of Morgana had the school crest above it in silver. The door itself had silver engravings all over the white ash. It was gorgeous and every time Mika had been in this ancient building she'd stopped here and wondered.

Most witches went to the University of Morgana. It wasn't required, but it was a rite of passage for most clans and high society. Mika had always known she would go one day and now here she was – finally.

A semester late.

And she wasn't a gifted witch. She was going in undeclared.

Claire had tried to tell her it was a mistake to go in undeclared, only the weakest witches went in without a specialty.

But there was no specialty for Mika. It didn't exist – not in the way that it did for her sister. Claire's five years were the best in her life she liked to say. She'd studied herbology and potions. There was nothing her sister didn't know about plants.

But Mika could never make the potions as well as Claire could. She did love the family greenhouse though – something she thought all witches could agree on.

"Mika."

She looked up and saw the High Priestess of the Bay Coven, Takahashi, standing next to her, hands clasped behind her back.

"Yes, High Priestess?"

"I'm glad you decided to go," Takahashi said gently. "I know things have been...difficult."

Mika still didn't know what she thought about the High Priestess or the promise the void witch had made to Takahashi.

Only Selene as High Priestess would get Kenzie Kavanagh to join the coven.

Personally, Mika thought it was best to have a void witch on her side, rather than not.

But Mika wasn't a normal witch. She'd come to learn that over the years.

"I appreciate the sentiment, High Priestess," Mika murmured, turning back to the door. "I will try to make our coven proud."

"May the Fates bless your journey," Takahashi said quietly. "And try to remember it's not always like this."

She nodded and placed her hand on the doorknob. The silver was cold – clearly enchanted. Mika twisted and pulled it open. The door was thick and heavy and instantly the freezing cold wind settled into her bones.

A male witch who looked to be in his mid to late twenties waited for her on the other side, dressed for the weather. "Welcome, Ms. Mika Marshall. Here, let me get your things."

"It's pronounced Mee-kah. Not Mike-ah." She was used to correcting people by this point in her life. No doubt she'd be doing it for the next five years as well.

"Of course, I apologize." The witch grabbed her trunk and she wondered if he always smiled so much.

Takahashi gave her one last nod and then disappeared into the depths of the coven building, snow trailing after her – so foreign in San Francisco.

Mika let the other witch take her trunk, but she held onto her suitcase, careful not to touch him. "Is the walk far?" she asked.

He shook his head and hefted the trunk onto his shoulder like it weighed nothing. Those broad shoulders of his no doubt helped some. "I'm one of the teaching assistants here. My name is Ryan."

She smiled slightly, just enough to be polite.

Smiling was exhausting. Mika couldn't remember the last time she'd smiled without doing it on purpose. Even before what happened with her father and brother...

Three years ago. That was the last time she'd smiled before everything had changed.

"You don't talk much do you?" Ryan asked. He smiled at her like it was the most natural thing in the world. He even laughed a little when she didn't answer. "Well, I'll take you to the admissions building where you can pick up your schedule and such. Classes start tomorrow. I'm surprised you didn't come last week."

Mika looked up at the university as it appeared through the trees. Her shoes didn't make any noise on the stone path and she wrapped her sweater tighter around her. "My mother's funeral was last week."

Instantly Ryan's smile dropped. "I'm so sorry. I heard about what had happened to the Bay Coven – hell, every witch has, but I didn't realize anyone had died."

"Heartbreak can do that to a person," she murmured, looking up, and then up.

The university was sprawling and absolutely gorgeous. It wasn't quite a castle, but close. An old luxurious estate that was just shy of a castle. It was all stone and gothic architecture and filled with presence. Mika could feel the magic that had seeped into it over the centuries.

The wrought iron gates swung open on their own as they approached and Mika wondered what it had been like last week when most had been arriving. Something else she was behind on. She would have to scramble to get ready and set up and try to find out where everything was.

Would she even be able to join any groups or clubs or teams?

Herbology 303: Advanced Poisons. Shifter Studies 101: An Introduction. Advanced Latin and Intermediate Sumerian. Runes: Past and Present. History of Magic 101 The Beginning of Magic, Science of Magic 304: Interdimensional Physics, and last but not least Hunting 204: Swordsmanship for the Hunter.

Eight goddamn classes to try and make up for starting a semester late. Most people took five and then a class or two in the summer. Some of the best classes were in the summer semesters when there were fewer students and specialties could really be focused on.

Of course one had to add their name to a list and hope the professor had enough participants for their specialty.

But Mika just wanted to make sure she graduated on time. She wanted to make sure that she could figure her damn life out before she had to leave, or decide if she wanted further training on a particular focus.

She sighed and adjusted her grip on her suitcase. She should have put her coat on like Claire had suggested that morning. But she'd been scatterbrained more than normal the last few months.

"Look, I'm really sorry about everything," Ryan said gently. "What happened last fall with your coven, it couldn't have been easy. So, if you need anything just let me know."

The massive wood doors to the university swung open as they approached and Mika nodded. "I appreciate that, Ryan. I think I can make my way from here."

He smiled down at her, but it was more subdued than when they first met. Mika tended to have that effect on people. "Can I give you my number? This place is massive. We could go the entire semester without seeing each other again, and I want to make sure you call me if you do ever need anything." Ryan smiled wider then and gently chucked her chin. "Not that you would ever admit you needed anything."

Mika blinked and a flare of panic at his touch rose and then died. She handed over her phone without even thinking – something about him made her instinctually want to trust him. At the very least he was observant, and he didn't push her into talking or...anything. Ryan was just there, offering his help without strings.

Which was exactly why she *didn't* trust him.

Mika didn't trust men the way she might have once, but having a teacher's assistant as a friend who knew the school much better than she probably wouldn't hurt. It was an alliance, nothing more.

"Thank you," she said, remembering her manners as he handed back her phone. "I appreciate the offer."

"Of course, Mee-kah Marshall," he said, over-pronouncing her name as he backed away. "Anything for Claire's sister." Then he turned the corner and disappeared.

And just like that her tiny bubble of good feeling was gone. She was just Claire's sister and he was being a good friend.

There was nothing about her that would make people remember her as just Mika. At least...nothing she was willing to show them.

"Ms. Marshall?" A woman in a cute pantsuit walked out of one of the offices and beckoned her to follow. "I've got your class list, your list of books, and your dorm mate waiting to meet you. I was so sorry to hear about your mother. You have our deepest condolences. We've done everything we can to make this transition easier on you."

Only because she was a Marshall. Mika highly doubted they did this for every student with a tragedy in the family.

Still, she followed the woman and grabbed the handle of her trunk. Mika could carry her own things despite everyone assuming she was incapable. It was just easier not to fight them when they offered.

"Mika Marshall?" a loud, female voice practically screeched from inside the admissions office.

She winced at the sound, but smoothed her features as she crossed into the brightly lit room. It still looked like a castle on the inside, but it had a bit of a homier feel – and it wasn't freezing. Her fingers began to thaw as she found the source of that voice.

"Is it true your ancestor was the first to discover gold in San Francisco?" the other witch asked.

"Audrey! I'm sorry, Ms. Marshall. Audrey is a bit...outgoing."

This was going to be a nightmare.

"Yes, that's true," Mika said. It was just easier to get this part out of the way. "Our family is very wealthy and has made many donations to the American branch of the University of Morgana."

Audrey inspected her closely, seeing more than Mika was comfortable with. "Cool. We're dorm mates. I'll help you get settled."

And that was that.

Mika blinked again as she took the papers with her list of classes and books. Wonders never ceased.

"Let's get your shit into the room and then we can get your books," Audrey said. "Need any help?"

"Audrey! I'm *so* sorry, Ms. Marshall," the admissions lady was saying. "I can find you another dorm..."

"This is fine, thank you," Mika said, interrupting the other woman. For the first time someone was giving her a choice and she wasn't about to throw that away. "I would love some help, Audrey. But I can take my trunk."

The other girl didn't smile. She just took the suitcase from Mika with narrowed eyes. She was perceptive.

Mika would have to be careful around her.

But she was also honest and straightforward. That was relieving.

After what had happened with her brother and father – Mika didn't feel like she could trust anyone anymore.

"I said I was coming here three weeks ago! Why is everyone losing paperwork?" A familiar voice practically screamed from the other room. "I swear to fucking Christ if you're doing this to keep me from attending I'm going to burn this place to the ground."

Mika craned her neck to try and see the other witch in the admissions cubicle. The university staff member helping her seemed flustered and...terrified.

"Kenzie," Selene's familiar voice whispered. "Calm down, they're not doing this on purpose."

"I just want to take one class so I can use the library.

This shouldn't be so hard," Kenzie grumbled. "I need some air."

Then she was up and stalking toward the exit, right toward Mika.

That red hair was a dead giveaway.

Kenzie stopped short when she recognized Mika and they stared at each other for a moment.

It felt like time slowed, dripping like sap from a maple tree in the dead of winter.

Mika remembered years ago when her parents had agreed to let her play with Selene at the Kavanagh mansion...back when everyone had avoided that place like the plague thanks to the 'abomination.' Going and spending the night had been...eye-opening.

What she'd seen and what she'd heard, well...*no one* should have to experience that. Not even her worst enemy should suffer what Kenzie had at the hands of her own family trying to 'fix' her.

"I'm not sorry about calling them out," Kenzie finally said to Mika, crossing her arms over her chest defensively.

But she did look a bit guilty. Mika didn't blame her though.

"Good," Mika murmured. "They all deserved it."

"But your mother didn't."

Audrey was a silent phantom next to her that Kenzie didn't even bother looking at.

"No," Mika agreed. "She didn't. But love isn't kind."

Kenzie tilted her head at that, about to open her mouth when Selene came up to them with that slight smile on her face – it seemed plastered on ever since she'd become matriarch.

If only Mika had been more powerful, maybe they would still be friends. She missed Selene.

Looking down at the floor out of respect for the strongest witch in their coven, Mika knew that at least Selene would make a good High Priestess one day. "Matriarch Kavanagh. It's a pleasure to see you again."

What she didn't expect was the massive sigh of relief. "Oh, thank the Fates you're here Mika. Will you help Kenzie when she's on campus for classes?"

Her grip tightened on her trunk. Would Selene ask that of her if she knew?

"You have my number, Matriarch." Still she didn't look up. Mika was a gnat in comparison to the power Selene could wield.

"Mika," Selene's gentle voice nearly broke her cool composure. "I'm sorry about your mother."

She looked up then, ignoring the tears that always welled in her eyes when someone actually meant the words they spoke to try and console her. "So am I. Call me if you ever need anything, Kenzie…Selene."

Then Mika turned and walked out of the admissions office with a surprisingly silent Audrey on her heels. The trunk was heavy but she barely felt it as she blindly walked away – anywhere but in that room with witches she knew and respected and had so much history with, who reminded her of everything that had happened.

If the future High Priestess of Bay Coven would take a void witch, would she take in Mika?

3

The dorm room was nicer than Mika expected. It was larger than her bedroom back home and they both had a full-sized bed instead of a twin. But she had to say, her favorite part was the massive bay windows with the plush velvet window seating.

Silvery light filtered in and she looked up at the sky. It looked like it might snow again.

The walls were made of stone and the wood to reinforce and insulate spoke to Mika. The aesthetic was perfect for this place, for her mood. Dark and mysterious – a place to learn about herself, because if she didn't people could die.

"I've already claimed the bed by the door. I hope that's all right," Audrey said, setting Mika's suitcase on the bare mattress. "Even if it's not, I'm not switching."

At least she was honest.

"Some guys came last week and replaced the mattress. Were they yours?"

Mika turned around and studied her new bed. "Yeah, my sister Claire arranged it." On top of all the preparations for their mother's funeral and grieving... Mika had done everything she could to help. Between the funeral, the requirements for the university, and keeping their grandmother alive, she had never felt more exhausted in her life than she had last week.

"The things money can do," Audrey said with a shake of her head. "I'm here on a scholarship. I was born into a middle class human family who doesn't believe in magic, so..." Audrey shrugged like it was no big deal, but they both knew it was.

Mika knew money made everything easier so she wouldn't bother trying to say something reassuring. "Then I guess whenever we go out it's my treat." It was all she could say or do really.

Audrey's smile finally came back at that. "Sounds good to me. Does that mean we're going to be friends?"

"Obviously." Mika opened her trunk and grabbed the brand new sheets on top. Being friends with the person who lived in the same room as her was smart – but she wondered if eventually Audrey would get tired of her once she realized just how boring Mika was.

"What's your specialty?" Audrey asked, flopping onto her own bed, looking up at the twinkling lights that framed her headboard.

And this was the part she'd been dreading. "I don't have a specialty. I'm undeclared."

The sheets fit perfectly of course – a deep sapphire blue so dark it looked almost black. Her sister had made sure they matched the school colors. That was so like Claire.

Audrey frowned. "Weird. I didn't know that was allowed. Are you just not sure what you want to focus on?"

"No, I just don't have a specialty."

Liar.

Mika ignored that whispery voice inside and took out the silver duvet, pillows, and the matching pillowcases. If Mary Poppins had owned a trunk this would be it.

"Really? Usually the old clans have really powerful witches."

"I know." There, the bed was made.

There were two armoires next to each other. Mika crossed the room and considered ordering a rug for the wood floor. Her armoire was empty other than a few basics her sister had probably arranged for her as well.

"So does that mean you're not very powerful?"

Audrey sure didn't have any issues with confrontation.

Mika finally stopped what she was doing and turned to face her dorm mate. This girl looked about her age, maybe a little younger. But it was the cold calculation in her eyes that impressed Mika. She was smart and tough as nails. Did she play the loud, outgoing schoolgirl to throw people off?

Without a word she grabbed the papers from her desk that contained everything she needed to start at the University of Morgana. Mika handed those over to Audrey and went back to setting up the armoire. No mini fridge, she would have to keep any snacks and drinks in the shared kitchen.

"Wow, I had no idea someone could score this low on the practical exam. Or this high on the theory. You're a weirdo," Audrey said with a laugh.

"You've no idea," Mika murmured. She slammed her armoire shut and grabbed her coat and warmer gloves. "I'll put my clothes away later. Would you like to come with me to buy my books?"

Audrey was still reading through Mika's papers, but she got to her feet and nodded. "Looks like we have some classes together. That's fortunate I guess. How the hell did you get into a hunter class?"

"I tested into it." Mika slipped on her elbow-length leather gloves with a sheepskin interior over the ones she already wore and then put on her wool pea coat that just brushed the tops of her boots. "Witches are traditionally physically weak. The Marshall matriarchs have always insisted that we train as hunters in tandem with our specialties. I assume it has something to do with our Wild West beginnings."

Audrey finally looked up and handed over the papers. "I see why you took mostly theory classes this year. And they're all so varied. But hey, you have hunting to fall back on if you need to right?"

Mika took the papers and studied the silvery crest at the top. It was a miracle she was here at all. She assumed there were two reasons they accepted her despite her test scores. The first being her family, and the second being the strange way her magic nearly disappeared three years ago.

Her grandmother wasn't in any condition to speak to the school, and Mika doubted Claire even really remembered. She suspected Takahashi had spoken to someone, maybe in hopes they would help uncover whatever her block was.

"I'm not as strong as a natural born hunter," Mika finally said. "But yeah, it's something."

Audrey had never taken off her coat. She grinned and stuck her hands in her pockets. "Would you like to walk around a bit first before we grab those doorstoppers?"

She had all day to explore the campus. Mika figured she should before having to deal with finding her classes and keeping up with the homework. This was supposed to be the best five years of her life after all.

Might as well maximize on it.

"Yeah, show me around," Mika said. "Show me everything Morgana has to offer."

"Well, we do have one of the best battle magic dodgeball teams in the world," Audrey said. "Tryouts for the Morgana Marauders are next week."

Mika's heart fluttered at that. So, she hadn't missed them. "Really?"

Who was she kidding? There was no way she could try out.

"Yeah," Audrey went on. "I'm going to try out, but I never had the opportunity to study battle magic so it's been a crash course since last summer." Audrey led her down the main hall to the large staircase. The outside walls were just glass so they could see the campus grounds and the forest beyond.

The common room on the bottom floor was empty, but it looked cozy. There were multiple fireplaces and overstuffed couches and chairs. Study tables were on one side and through another door she could see their dorm's kitchen.

Oleander House was bought and paid for by the Marshall clan almost a hundred years ago. And the dormitory was just as lovely as all the brochures stated. Fitting name, she supposed. The women in her family had always been obsessed with poisonous flowers and plants.

Mika pushed open the great big oak door and sighed when she realized she'd forgotten her scarf. Living in the frozen north was going to take some getting used to. The air was biting and cold and the snow on the ground crunched.

"Have you seen the Morgana stadium for battle magic dodgeball?" Audrey asked as they headed down one of the stone paths.

"I haven't." Mika wondered if she would ever get the guts to try out. Just thinking about it made her sick to the stomach, a strange flutter in her belly and a shaking in her hands. Having that many people watching her – waiting for her to fail...

It would be for the best if she didn't.

"Let's go there first while it's still light outside," Audrey suggested. "It gets darker here faster than you think it would in the winter. You blink and all of a sudden it's pitch black."

Mika glanced sideways at her dorm mate and considered her. She was smart. And clearly gifted at something or she wouldn't be here on a scholarship. She was interested in battle magic dodgeball – the most dangerous witch sport in existence. Which meant she was an adrenaline junkie, or in it for the glory.

Audrey was one of those naturally gorgeous girls. She had this thick brown hair that seemed red in the sunlight, and these full pink lips that looked like what people would take pictures of to their plastic surgeons.

Her eyes were blue, but not cold like Mika's. They were bright and clear with this ring of green that really set off her freckles. Audrey was shorter than most witches, but not by much. They were actually almost the same exact height.

Absolutely gorgeous.

Mika would have to see what she would do with that beauty over the semester. People like Audrey...either they used it to get what they wanted, or they used it to get as many boys as they possibly could – a boyfriend stealer.

Or maybe she was just one of those rare few who were just glad she wasn't ugly.

"I can train you," Mika said softly, looking around to make sure no one could overhear them.

"In battle magic?" Audrey asked, eyebrows shooting up in surprise. "Your practical is shit, no offense. I wouldn't think you could do battle magic."

Mika cleared her throat and followed Audrey

through the forest to the stadium looming in the distance. "They don't test for battle magic on the practical exam."

"Holy shit," Audrey laughed. "So you do have a specialty!"

It wasn't her specialty, but Mika kept her mouth shut about it and let Audrey think what she wanted.

"I don't want other people to know," Mika murmured. "Witches are neutral. You know that. There hasn't been a warrior witch for centuries."

"Since Morgana le Fay," Audrey mused. "You think she'd be disappointed in what we've become?"

"Do you want the training or not?" Mika asked, trying not to panic when she saw people gathering as the trees thinned and the stadium came into view.

"Of course! That will really help, thanks Mika." Audrey sped up and pulled her towards the stadium. "Now let's see last year's team. I heard the boys train with their shirts off even in the dead of winter. 'Character building' or something like that."

Mika thought it sounded idiotic, but she didn't say anything about it, and just barely managed to keep up with Audrey.

Despite everything she liked her dorm mate. And if training her for a week put Mika in her good graces... maybe it would make the next five years easier on both of them.

4

The stadium was just as old and gothic as the actual university. Mika followed Audrey inside to sit in the bleachers and watch. What surprised her was how many people were there just to observe the players training. Maybe they were all bored after the Welcome Back Week festivities.

Twenty people were on the platform going through different strategies together. Mika saw that the water surrounding that platform was covered with metal plating. She could still hear the slosh of water and see it through the metal mesh. Falling into that in the winter would be brutal.

"So you've played before?" Audrey asked, scooting closer so she could whisper into Mika's ear.

Mika nodded and noticed one of the players was actually shirtless. What an idiot. But...she could see why. A gaggle of girls sat as close to the field as they could, giggling as they watched the players.

"Why aren't there more girls on the team?" Mika asked.

It was a co-ed sport. Seemed weird to her there was only one girl.

"A girl *died* last semester," Audrey whispered. "I guess they thought she could swim and when she got knocked off the platform into the water she just...drowned."

Mika just barely managed to refrain from rolling her eyes. "That doesn't explain why there aren't more female witches on the team. And who the hell is the coach that they didn't *ask* if their players can swim?"

Something wasn't adding up. Had whatever infected her coven made it to this place as well?

Maybe she was just jumping to conclusions.

"There is no coach," Audrey said, giving her a funny look. "At university level the captain of the team runs things."

Mika studied the biggest, and of course shirtless, male player. His dark brown skin shone under the winter sun. "Him?" she asked, pointing.

"Yeah, that's Malachi," Audrey told her. "He's the youngest captain in fifty years. He's only a year ahead of us."

They watched in silence as the team huddled and then ran scrimmages, splitting up to play against each other. The magic flared and exploded. The crowd gasped and cheered like they would if it was an actual game.

Mika watched Malachi closely, but he seemed innocent enough. An all American boy, from the

Midwest no doubt for him to get that kind of musculature and actually be able to use it. He watched out for his teammates and shielded them when he could.

And he was beautiful. Dark brown skin, rippling muscles, and piercing eyes...Mika refocused on the actual game.

Even when the players on the opposite side were hit with something hard enough to fling them into what would have been the water had it been uncovered, he'd stop and make sure they were okay, dodging attacks the whole time.

A natural born leader.

Did he think men should rule covens?

Mika tapped her finger on the bench.

If men were as powerful as women in magic she could understand it. But hundreds of years ago there were just a handful of male witches. They went by wizards then, but...there was a reason the university was named after Morgana and not Merlin.

Mika wondered sometimes...what would the world look like today if they hadn't been called pagans and evil doers and shoved into hiding.

The world used to be accepting of magic, but not anymore.

And now the human culture was poisoning theirs. She supposed she should be grateful they'd held it off for as long as they had.

"He's in our Shifter Studies class," Audrey told her, giving Mika a look. "Do you think he's hot?"

"I was actually wondering if he'd killed that girl for a

modicum more of power," Mika snapped, irritated everything always had to be about boys.

This wasn't the way to make friends. Lashing out wasn't going to help her in the long run.

"Geez, I was just asking." Audrey's voice was too loud.

Mika had to leave or she was going to say something else she would regret. Standing up made her hands shake as it felt like everyone in the stadium turned to look at her. Even the players stopped to see what was going on.

"Look, I didn't mean to make you uncomfortable," Audrey said, grabbing her hand so she was stuck in place.

Mika yanked her hand out of Audrey's and started to panic as the moment went on indefinitely – as murmurs grew louder.

"Hey! Is everything okay?" Malachi called up from the field, jogging over to the ledge.

Mika hoped the girl would forgive her later. But she couldn't let anyone touch her. She had to get out of here.

"Audrey, you okay?" Malachi asked.

Of course they knew each other well enough for him to ask her directly. This just kept getting better and better. Mika tried to get around Audrey but the girl was a fucking rock so Mika was trapped between her and a hard place.

She was going to end up looking like a full on bitch if she couldn't get out of here before someone directed the conversation toward her.

"Oh yeah, this is my dorm mate," Audrey called back. "She's going to train me in battle magic."

Aaaaaand there it was.

Fucking fuck.

Everyone stopped what they were doing to stare at her. Her white-blonde hair was a dead giveaway – 'look at me!' Maybe she should dye it black.

"Really?" Malachi asked. "I thought you were going to train with us, Audrey."

Mika was amazed he hadn't instantly turned the conversation to her. It gave her the opportunity to start walking away.

Audrey grabbed her hand again and the grip was surprisingly strong. Yank away too hard and she might just send the other witch tumbling down the bleachers.

Her hands started to tingle as she became more panicked and Mika felt bile rise in her throat. "Please, let go, Audrey," she whispered. "I don't want to hurt you."

Then the shirtless boy—really, he was a man—made it to their seats. Mika pulled her hand out of Audrey's as the other witch stood to hug Malachi.

"Is she going to be your new girlfriend?" Malachi asked, eyeing Mika up and down as she rubbed her hands on her coat.

Thank the Fates she'd been wearing gloves.

Audrey smiled and gave Malachi a little push. "Well, if she was, she's probably not going to now that you've said that."

Mika turned and stared at Audrey. Well...she'd read all those signs wrong. Had Audrey just been flirting with her and she'd missed it, or was she trying to cover for her now?

"What do you say?" Malachi studied her closer than Mika would prefer.

"Aren't you cold?" she asked instead, purposefully keeping her eyes on his face.

"I don't need a wing man Malachi, for fuck sake." Audrey pushed him again and he gave Audrey a kiss on the cheek.

It was fucking adorable.

"I hope to see you both at tryouts then," Malachi said, giving Mika a wink. "But no canoodling during my practices."

Then he was jogging back down to the field and Mika felt like she could breathe again. Instantly she was climbing the stairs up to the top of the stadium seating so she could get the hell out of this place.

For the last three years she'd done everything she could to become nothing – to become invisible. Mika didn't like people looking too closely at her – what if they saw? What if they could somehow tell there was something wrong with her deep down?

"Mika! I'm sorry about that," Audrey called, running after her. "Girl, slow down. I'm not going to try and turn you gay or anything."

Despite having the intense urge to clarify she didn't care about that at all, Mika sped up and practically ran down the stairs on the other side of the hall. Damn stadium was built like a maze. She just wanted to get *out*.

Coming here had been a mistake. She should have stayed home – taken online herbology classes. Tending the family greenhouse could be her thing. That's how she could earn her keep. Mika had always been really good with the poisonous plants and flowers.

Her green thumb was even better than her sister's.

"Mika!"

The only way Audrey could catch up with her was...

Dammit, she was lost.

"Hey! I didn't mean to make things extra awkward, but you were being *super* weird and I just don't get it. Hey, are you okay?" Audrey asked, grabbing Mika's arms to steady her.

"Where are we? Stop touching me!"

The look of hurt that crossed Audrey's face was like a slap. Mika bent over and put her hands on her knees. She breathed deep, trying to soothe the panic attack before it became too much for her to handle.

"It's not you," Mika whispered. "I promise. Just...give me a minute."

Audrey didn't say anything but she didn't leave either.

So many people staring at her shouldn't have set her off so badly. But if they knew...if they knew how good she was at battle magic they would wonder about the rest of her magic. Why couldn't she light a candle without needing to catch her breath? Why did she avoid using magic whenever possible? *Why* was she so good at offensive magic?

What else was she hiding?

All because Mika wanted to make friends and be a

normal witch at a university that was supposed to make all her dreams come true.

"Hey, it's okay. Whatever it is, it's okay." Audrey didn't touch her though, and Mika was grateful for that.

It gave her the strength to stand and she took one last cleansing breath. "It's not you," Mika repeated, shoving her gloved hands in her coat pockets. "I have anxiety. Getting called out like that in front of so many people set it off. I'm...a very private person normally."

Audrey still looked hurt, her arms crossed over her chest.

She needed to clarify or this was going to ruin any chance they had at friendship.

"I wouldn't date you, not because you're a girl," Mika said. "But because I don't want to date anyone. Plus... we're dorm mates. If it didn't work out it would be weird."

Audrey slowly smiled. "You're not even my type," she teased. "Malachi just has zero gaydar and makes assumptions. Don't worry, I know you're mostly straight."

Mika breathed a sigh of relief and the tingling in her hands started to fade. "I still want to train you, but I have no plans of trying out for the team."

"Whatever you want, weirdo. If you're up for it, then just let me know what sets off your anxiety. I'll do what I can." Audrey bumped her shoulder with hers. "The dorms are back that way," she said with a jerk of her chin. "But the bookstore is that way – where the main university is. Let's go get your books and then watch Bewitched."

She couldn't help but laugh. "Okay," Mika agreed. "That sounds good."

Maybe this hadn't been a mistake after all.

5

M ika leaned against one of the tables in the massive greenhouse and watched as students filtered in. There weren't many taking Advanced Poisons but the ones who were, were fascinating.

The first two classes of the day had gone pretty well. Audrey had both Advanced Latin and Shifter Studies with her on Mondays and Wednesdays. But she was alone in her Poisons class.

The other witch was great at diverting attention away from Mika since she already knew so many people with as outgoing as she was. They were fairly normal first days – a general reviewing of the schedule and then getting right into it. None of the classes Mika was taking were easy.

But she could already tell this class was going to be different.

It was quiet in the conservatory with the black metal

scrollwork holding the glass in place. The massive greenhouse was nearly an entire wing of the university and three stories tall. Mika knew this was going to be one of her favorite places.

The humidity was suffocating in her coveralls. But handling these kinds of plants required her to take safety measures. It was something she'd been taught from the moment she'd been able to walk. Wear clothes that could be washed and covered every inch of skin.

Mika had her black coveralls that she'd brought from home on over her regular clothes, boots that sealed the coveralls and didn't allow anything to touch her skin, special gloves that could be washed but protected her from any oils that might be secreted from the plants. A scarf around her neck would cover her nose and mouth if they had to do any cutting or crushing – it was generally a good idea, even just smelling some poisonous plants could make someone faint.

Everything else was in the locker rooms specifically set up for herbology students. Cream that protected skin was everywhere, both magical and non. This portion of the greenhouse was under lock and key; only students with a pass or teachers could access these plants.

She surveyed the other students and dismissed them immediately. All except one.

Honestly, she was surprised to see a male witch in this class. Most never made it to Advanced Poisons. It wasn't really their thing. But this one – he was tall and mysterious. So tall he would probably tower about a foot over her.

Mika had a weakness for tall guys.

His gorgeous brown hair was messy and slightly curled, falling in his face just a little. The green in his light-bluish green eyes seemed magnified with all the plants around him. Mika couldn't help but notice how muscular his arms were with the way his coveralls hung from his waist, showing off his tank top.

Despite her vow to avoid men and any potential boyfriends throughout her university career, Mika's heart started beating just a little bit faster. When he looked up, his gaze went right to her like he knew she'd been watching him, her stomach flipped and Mika had to look away.

She glanced at her watch. Only two more minutes and the class would start.

Professor Hayes waltzed in a minute later in custom coveralls that looked a lot like Mika's just in a faded green instead. The professor had her long blonde hair up in a severe bun and she wore glasses. There would be no room for bullshit with her.

Mika looked up at the glass ceiling as the silvery light filtering in seemed to change somehow. She blinked and realized it was snowing. It had been a long time since she'd been around snow, and the way it fell in whispers on the glass added to the magic of the conservatory.

"Welcome class. The reason you are here is because you've either met the pre-requisites or you've tested into this class. Congratulations. Most never make it this far." Professor Hayes had a hard gleam in her eye as she studied each of them.

It was like she was assessing who was going to mess up and potentially kill themselves, or perhaps someone else.

"People have died in this class. Murderers have used what is learned here. I guarantee you'll end up with some kind of burn at the very least. So if you want to make it out alive you listen to me and follow the rules. Do you understand?"

Mika nodded, remembering a similar conversation her mother had had with her when she was about five and touched a plant that had left a burn mark for weeks. "Be smart, Mika," she'd said. "If you're not smart, you'll die."

It was advice she'd taken to heart and applied to her entire life. Mika had made sure she was smart. Even if she had to study twice as hard as everyone else. She wasn't going to make a stupid mistake and die.

Not when it was *so* easy to end up dead.

"Any questions?"

"Professor Hayes?" some quiet girl with black hair asked. "Will there be opportunities for extra credit?"

Mika couldn't stop herself from rolling her eyes. Couldn't they get on with this already?

"We'll see," the professor said, eyeing the girl like she'd probably be the first to head to the infirmary. "Now I'm going to pair you up, and you will be partners for the rest of the semester. We're going to start with every day poisonous plants and flowers and their uses."

Professor Hayes took her phone out of her pocket and read off names. Mika felt that same flutter in her stomach when her name was called and the professor pointed to the guy who had caught her attention. "Mika Marshall, you're with Ethan Ellington."

She didn't even have the opportunity to be shocked that the professor had pronounced her name correctly. Ethan was already headed toward her and the way he looked at her...it was almost a glare but not quite.

Somehow it made him even more attractive.

He didn't say anything as he jerked his chin toward one of the work tables. Mika followed after him and wondered what his deal was. Maybe he was annoyed she was a freshman. This was a higher level class after all. Freshmen weren't usually allowed.

But they'd made an exception for her of course – she was a Marshall with an affinity for poison.

"Now, we're going to start with Morning Glory. It's toxic, but it doesn't usually kill. The fascinating thing about the Morning Glory is it's one of those flowers that can cause hallucinations. The seeds contain a chemical similar to that of LSD." The professor walked around the greenhouse, setting pots of the flower on each worktable.

Mika sat on the stool and ignored Ethan next to her as best as she could. She forced herself to pay attention to the professor, even though this was hardly advanced.

Hopefully they'd get into more dangerous plants as the semester went on.

"You don't need to wear gloves for these, but I advise you scrub down after every class. Now," Professor Hayes snapped, whipping around to study Mika.

What she'd done to gain her attention she had no idea.

"Morning glory is used in a few different types of spells and potions. The most popular is an infusion, but philtres are also common. Ms. Marshall, name one for me."

She must have seen Mika's test scores. Professor Hayes was one of the more strict professors or so Mika had heard, but she was also one of the best. Had she known she'd be instantly singled out...maybe she would have avoided this class.

"Obfusca," she murmured. "It makes a person confused if made with sea water. If the potion is made with river water it can remove memories. Officially, it is not a curse, but it's also not a healing potion."

The professor narrowed her eyes and then smiled. "I'm pleased to see you're just as good as your test results indicated. Welcome to Morgana, Ms. Marshall."

Too many people were looking at her.

Mika dropped her gaze to the flower and its deep purple petals. Ethan chose just then to lean in closer to her. Instantly she stiffened as the scent of his cologne reached her nose.

"Who are you here to kill?" he whispered.

What?

Her eyes snapped to his and there was laughter there, like this was some hilarious joke. "Excuse me?"

"Normal people don't take Advanced Poisons in their first semester." Ethan pulled out a sketchbook and started drawing the morning glory. "Unless it's your specialty I guess."

"It's not." Mika couldn't believe how green his eyes looked in this light, and how even in the dead of winter his skin was still slightly tanned. "But it's one of the few things I'm good at."

Ethan smiled at that, glancing at her as he drew. "I'm an Herbology major. Is the Marshall Greenhouse in San Francisco as amazing as I hear?"

So he did know who she was. Ugh, Mika wished she could just be a normal witch for once. But high society witches all knew each other. Which meant Ethan wasn't from the West Coast. So who was he?

Ellington wasn't a familiar clan name either.

Why herbology?

"So who are *you* here to kill?" she asked, plucking one of the flowers as instructed so she could separate the parts.

"I just like plants. There's something so beautiful in something that has such variance. Some are deadly and some can save you. Only knowledge can tell you which one." Ethan smiled at her then and there was something about the way his hair fell into his eyes.

Mika wanted to reach out and brush it back, maybe trace those glorious eyebrows, and his unfairly long eyelashes.

Fuck.

This wasn't why she was here.

She went back to placing the petals in one bowl and

the seeds in another. Two different potions – one to take something away, and one to give something back. There was beauty in the duality, she'd give Ethan that.

His poetic ass was going to be the death of her if she didn't pay attention.

The class was two hours long and they went through the basic poisonous flowers, how to handle them, what they could be used for, and how one would prepare them as ingredients for future use. Mika went through the motions, doing her best to ignore Ethan next to her.

It was all basic stuff she knew anyway. Her mother had taught her all this and more by the time she was ten. Their greenhouse had a poison garden just like this one did. It rivaled some of the greats around the world.

"Don't worry, we're supposed to learn how to grow and tend nightshade and hemlock this semester," Ethan said with a little smirk. "Morning glory is pretty tame in comparison."

How boring. Mika was hoping they'd get to work with the Manchineel tree, fondly nicknamed the 'little apple of death.' It was one of the few her mother hadn't let her near since it could blister skin in seconds.

Snakeroot and oleander were also some of her favorites, but Mika had been hoping for something truly exotic.

"I heard someone is trying to crossbreed poisons," Ethan murmured. "Would that be more interesting for you?"

Mika whipped her gaze to his and narrowed her eyes. "You think I'm some kind of black widow?"

"I think you like dangerous things." Ethan didn't blink as he held her gaze. "Am I wrong?"

She didn't say anything to that. They didn't even know each other. Mika owed him no explanation.

But he wasn't wrong.

6

T he piece of paper in her pocket had been difficult to ignore. Mika supposed she could have left it in her dorm room, but something had compelled her to keep it on her person.

After her Advanced Poisons class, she'd gone to change and the morning glory Ethan drew had fallen out of the pocket on her coveralls. The flower was exquisitely done and in perfect detail. And so were her studious profiles.

Mika had nearly tossed it in the fireplace, but something about the way he saw her kept her from doing it.

Seeing herself through someone else's eyes was rare and she'd only ever really seen it once in a photograph taken by her ex-boyfriend. In his eyes she was ethereal, fairy-like, and she'd been laughing in the watery springtime sun.

Ethan's drawing was a totally different version of her

Mika didn't know if she was ready to accept. He saw her as angry by the glare on her face – how she narrowed her eyes at the plant. But somehow he'd also captured the fear and grief she usually hid in one of those profiles – one where he'd caught her giving him a sideways glance.

Mika held the paper in her pocket and tried to focus on interdimensional physics, but it was a lost cause. And this was no easy first week. Each class had jumped right into the meat of the subject.

"Everything okay?" Ryan asked, setting a quiz down on her desk. "You seem distracted."

Mika looked up into those devastating blue eyes and recognized the guy who'd welcomed her to the university. His black hair was shaggy like Ethan's but straight, and he wasn't as tall, but...those shoulders.

Was this seriously the girl she was going to be? The girl who was won over with some pretty eyes or a drawing?

"I'm fine," Mika snapped. "What are you even doing here?"

Ryan's dark eyebrows shot up but he didn't say anything about her attitude. He just pushed the quiz closer. "I TA for this class. Good luck, Mika." Then he turned and walked down the stairs toward the podium where the professor was explaining how he just wanted to see where they were on the basics.

Mika ignored the other students near her who were eyeing her like she was a bitch and took out her favorite pen. Her father gave it to her when she'd graduated high school. She kept it to remind her everything was a lie – even a kind gesture.

And yet there were people in this university who seemed bound and determined to prove her wrong.

Audrey at least she believed for the most part. Mika was still wary of that girl. They barely knew each other, and until she knew what made Audrey tick she could still be surprised by something the other witch might do.

Sighing and starting on the first question, she tried not to think how badly witch society had fucked her up.

The reason Selene was so normal and nice was Kenzie had mostly raised her.

Mika had Claire, but not really. Claire had always been into her own stuff. Her sister loved witch society. She loved the parties and the hierarchy and the power their clan wielded. It was a miracle she wasn't a total bitch.

Their mother had done a good job – but it was always their clan against the world. She'd sown distrust into them very young. Other witch clans would always want what they had – or so she'd said.

Mika chewed on her lip and frowned. These questions were hard. Basics her ass.

She pulled out her calculator and started running the equations for building a portal from this plane to hell, large enough to transport two people at once.

This was the kind of magic she loved. It was hard, but safe and predictable. If she got it right the spell would work exactly the way it was supposed to every time.

Physics could be bent and remade with a few runes and the right equation – but there was always an answer.

It wasn't like her 'gift' at all.

Ten questions later she was done. Mika looked up and saw she was the first to finish.

There was no way she was going to be the first to get up after her little scene. She sighed again and wished she could get her shit together. Was there a tincture for that? Maybe a charm.

Someone else stood up and Mika used that opportunity to do so as well. It was easier to hide if she wasn't the only one moving. In a class of thirty she still felt conspicuous. But there were other high society clan witches here. They just seemed far more at home than she did.

Maybe if she wasn't the only Bay Coven witch in the freshman class it would feel less weird.

No one knew what it was like to have their coven ripped apart by betrayal – by the males they trusted the most in the world.

If she couldn't trust her father and brother – what man could she trust?

Ryan smiled at her as she set the quiz on the professor's desk where he sat and instantly started grading it. "If you wait a second I can get this back to you right now."

Mika glanced at the other student and saw him waiting while the professor graded his at the podium. If this was the norm, waiting would bring less attention to her. The last thing she needed was someone else to ask her what her specialty was.

Not that saying anything would help. There were no classes on what she could do – not really. Mika had already looked.

"This is excellent work," Ryan told her, sounding impressed. "Your methodology is a bit different than what we teach here, but it's effective. Who taught you?"

"My father," she murmured, taking the quiz back from him. "98%? Why not 100% if I got all the questions correct?"

"Your first answer assumed both people were witches. You didn't account for anyone who might be larger, like a shifter. It's always best to make sure a portal has more room than required – though I have to say your equations are extremely precise. It's just rare you'll know the exact height and weight of each person."

Ryan smiled up at her and Mika was instantly drowning in those inky blue depths.

Stupid hormones.

She turned and made her way back up the stairs to her spot in the very back. The wooden desks were old and made of ash. The blue velvet seating looked like it had been replaced recently as well as the stuffing.

The stadium seating was in a semi-circle around the platform placed at the very bottom, and then cut into three sections so there was minimal climbing over other people. She watched Ryan sitting at the professor's desk, grading quizzes as they were brought down to him. Professor Temples was doing the same at the podium.

It hadn't snowed yet today, but it was darker than it should have been for a midday class. The wood and stone gothic architecture was Mika's constant mood. It was dark and gloomy and loomed over everything in this place, but it was also beautiful in a heart wrenching romantic kind of way.

Like every romantic tragedy was steeped into the stone itself.

She looked at Ryan's handwriting on her quiz. It was barely legible, but confident and sure in his corrections. On the last page he'd written a little note: 'You can apologize for your attitude with a muffin the next time I see you.'

Mika slammed the paper down and crossed her arms over her chest. She wanted to glare at Ryan from across the classroom but that wouldn't make anyone think she was any less crazy and Mika didn't want rumors spreading about her and Ryan.

Asshole had basically demanded a date and an apology in the same breath. Assumptive prick.

She pulled out her phone and texted Audrey. Anything to distract herself from the hottie sneaking looks at her.

Ryan looked up at her again. Mika wondered what he saw.

Did he see the sad girl hiding in fear? Or did he see something else entirely?

Professor Temples adjusted his glasses and smiled up at them. "Let's begin."

7

"Did you know that the cemetery on the island was here before the school was?" Audrey asked as they made their way from the dorms through the trees. "It dates all the way back to the Vikings."

Mika hunched her shoulders against the cold and buried her face in her scarf. "It's weird they even have a cemetery here since witches are cremated."

Snow crunched under their boots, but otherwise it was silent. Occasionally Mika could hear the hoot of an owl, but this deep into winter there wasn't much wildlife out and about. Plus there was something about this cemetery – the very air had some kind of essence she couldn't put her finger on.

"The university pays for the John and Jane Doe's to be buried here so we can use their bones and bodies for various different spells and such." Audrey shrugged like it was no big deal, but glanced over her shoulder as they got closer.

Essentially buying dead bodies legally was creepy. Effective, but creepy.

Mika stopped when the trees thinned almost suddenly, like there was a line she couldn't see. Headstones and crypts dotted the clear acre of land like small, stone trees. That weird feeling grew stronger, almost like the air was stale despite being outside. She could practically taste the bone dust.

Wrinkling her nose, she glanced sideways at Audrey. "Are you ready?"

The other witch nodded and pulled her shoulder-length hair back into a ponytail. "Yeah, I've been practicing."

Mika checked the space one last time. "Do you want to put up a shield or something?"

Audrey glanced at her then. There was that suspicion. But she didn't say anything. One of these days she was going to. Mika knew it was only a matter of time. Because despite being in four classes together she'd never seen Mika do magic.

And people did magic at the university *all* the time.

"Yeah I can do that, good idea." Audrey twisted her fingers in the correct pattern and whispered a few words. It was rather simple, but Audrey had so much power that Mika could feel the strength in the shield. Not many would be able to get through it.

"For someone born outside a clan you've got more magic than most witches I've met," Mika told her. "It'll help make this place easier to bear I'm sure."

Audrey shrugged and gave her a half smile. "Having such a prestigious witch for a friend helps too."

Mika didn't smile back, but she knew it was true no matter how much she hated it. Audrey would always be an outsider until she joined a coven, and even then... "If people are assholes tell me. It's against school policy to discriminate and a little belladonna goes a long way."

Her dorm mate didn't laugh. She just nodded, because they'd both learned enough about each other over the last three days to know...Mika knew how to make someone suffer without killing them.

"Now, show me what you can do." Mika pulled one glove off. "We're going to do a little one on one." Then she pulled off the other and set them on top of a nearby headstone. "We have a few hours before my swordsmanship class. Will you meet me after so we can head to Sumerian together?"

"Are you kidding? I'm totally sitting in on that class." Audrey laughed and started drawing runes in the air. A quick twist and the lines now glowed in the snow, creating a temporary field. "But yeah, I'll walk you to Sumerian. The language wing is clear across campus. Your little thirty minute window is going to bite you in the ass one day."

"Probably," Mika agreed. "You know the three shields allowed for blocking right?"

"Duh." Audrey rolled her eyes. "That's always the first thing taught."

"For a good reason." Mika flexed her fingers and rolled her head to the right and then to the left, loosening up the tight muscles. Her anxiety was trying to rear its ugly head, but no one was going to be touching her and Audrey was more powerful than she was when it came to shields.

The main reason Mika didn't want to join the team other than her little issue – even though she still desperately wanted to tryout just to see if she was good enough – was because her defensive magic was shit. Anything that was considered 'neutral,' 'benign,' or 'defensive' and she froze up. Part of it was her fear, and part of it was she could never get in the right head space.

"First hit and the round is done. Follow the rules, and try not to accidentally kill me," Mika told Audrey.

Just by the way the other witch was standing Mika knew she would have to shield first, but her hunter training was good for many things.

"Ready?" Audrey asked, twisting her fingers to create a clock for round one.

"Don't hold back." Mika knew the other witch was nervous. She could practically smell it. Audrey had never seen her do a spell. Very few had, and that made most witches very nervous.

A snap of Audrey's fingers and the bell clanged in the empty clearing.

Audrey came at her with an offensive spell, but Mika had been expecting it. She spun to the left and twisted her fingers in the right shape and threw the spell hard – no words spoken. The look of shock on Audrey's face when she just barely got her shield up in time told Mika everything she needed to know.

Her dorm mate hadn't believed she could throw battle magic.

Mika wasn't mad about it. She never performed magic for a reason.

When Audrey's shield cracked Mika stopped, waiting for the other witch to regain her bearings. Mika could have decimated her in less than three moves, but that wasn't the point of this exercise.

"What was that spell?" Audrey asked, wiping her broken shield away. "You didn't say a word. It takes mad focus and power to throw a spell without the incantation. I wasn't even sure you could *do* magic."

For the first time in a long time Mika grinned, but it wasn't out of joy. "I know." Two movements of her fingers and she threw another attack.

Audrey deflected the fire and came back with a crackling ball of energy. Mika didn't bother deflecting or shielding. Instead she caught the spell and whispered three words, compressing it into a smaller ball – molding it, shifting it, forcing it to bend beneath her will.

Then she threw it back.

It exploded against Audrey's shield and the other witch flew back almost ten feet before hitting the ground and skidding to a stop against a headstone.

"What the *fuck*!"

Mika was already running. She hopped over one headstone and dodged another. "Are you okay?" she asked, dropping to her knees and running her hands over the other witch, careful not to make skin to skin contact.

"I thought your shield would hold up better than that. I'm so sorry."

But Audrey wasn't mad. She was laughing her ass off.

"Holy shit girl, why the hell aren't you trying out?"

Mika sat back on her heels in annoyance. "I was actually worried about you."

That made Audrey laugh even harder.

"I could have really hurt you." Mika crossed her arms over her chest and glared as the other witch propped herself up on her elbows in the snow.

"Oh you definitely can. Which is why it's so fucking funny, dude. You walk around like this weeping willow incapable of doing a basic spell such as lighting a candle and here you are, nearly blowing me to pieces. No wonder you don't want people touching you." Audrey was still laughing as she got to her feet and Mika didn't know what to say.

"It's not that simple," Mika muttered.

"Clearly. You've got some serious shit going on, but you aren't a delicate flower babe. And *that* is what's so funny. You've got everyone fooled and I love it." Audrey got to her feet and dusted the snow from her clothes. "What are you hiding from?"

"You wouldn't understand." Mika slipped her hands into her pockets. "I'm not *acting* like I can't do basic magic. I can't even properly shield."

Mika said a few words and made a small cross over her chest – the first basic shield they taught. It popped up in front of her and it was so thin she could see right through it to Audrey. Not only that, the effort to keep it from disintegrating made her winded.

She fluttered her fingers to make the shield dissipate and took a moment to catch her breath, staring up at the dark clouds in the sky. Did it ever stop snowing here?

"That's weird," Audrey said, studying her in that way again. Like there was something Mika was hiding.

Which she was.

"What happened?" Audrey asked.

Mika finally met Audrey's gaze. Could she trust this girl? Could she maybe end up being a *real* friend? "What makes you think something happened?"

Audrey leaned against one of the headstones and crossed one ankle over the other, hands in her coat pockets. "I grew up in the human world, hiding who I was. My parents didn't know until puberty hit and I couldn't hide it any more. My magic flared – finally at full strength. I know everyone says your abilities are locked in at five, but we're witches. Puberty is when we become a woman and I fully believe *that* is when our powers are fully manifested. Specialties are usually noticed around then as well – from everything I've read at least."

Audrey squinted at Mika. "I have an affinity for enchantments. I can spell objects in my sleep. When I told my mom...she committed me to a psych ward and I spent four years in that place. I couldn't get out until I was eighteen. The dean of the university signed me out herself and I've been living here since. I don't know how they track these things – magic in witches born to humans, but I've never been more grateful to anyone in my life."

Her hands shook and Mika felt sick to her stomach. Living among witches was bad, but being committed for trusting the person you loved most? They really were kindred souls. "What happened when you were committed?"

"I couldn't do any magic for six months." Audrey cocked her head and studied Mika. "Lighting a candle made me faint from the amount of energy I had to expend. Then, ironically, one day in therapy my therapist told me I was afraid of what I was capable of. She was talking about normal mundane shit obviously."

Mika felt her heart thundering in her chest. No wonder this girl looked at her the way she did. She *knew*. Maybe not the details, but she knew Mika was hiding and why.

"I realized I was terrified of my magic after the reaction I got," Audrey said. "And once I accepted it, I could light a candle without even thinking."

Mika walked away, practically stomping in the snow. "It's not that simple."

"What are you so afraid of?" Audrey called after her. "I didn't peg you as a coward."

"You couldn't possibly understand," Mika snapped, whipping around. "What happened...what I did...it wouldn't get me committed, but it could get my powers stripped at the very least."

Audrey blinked at that and shoved off the headstone. "Must be some intense shit then."

They stood two feet apart from each other, neither blinking. Mika wanted to trust her. She really did. But there was still so much she didn't know about her.

At least Audrey wasn't tied to a clan. That made it easier to trust the other witch. There were no other loyalties, except maybe to the dean of the university.

"In my coven, there was a man named Bradley Davis," Mika said quietly. "At the time he was well respected – studying to be a lawyer and pretty powerful considering he was male."

Audrey crossed her arms over her chest but didn't say anything.

"I didn't know back then, but I wasn't the only one." Mika had to look away from Audrey. If there was pity or disgust on the other witch's face – Mika may just do something she would regret. "I was sixteen and had just gotten my first period. My magic was finally fully mature."

She remembered how excited she'd been. The Beltane celebration had felt like it was especially for her. Mika had never felt so sure of herself in her life. Everything had been perfect.

"After the coven's Beltane celebrations Bradley pulled me aside and I thought...honestly I had no idea what I thought but it never occurred to me he would try to hurt me." Mika looked down at her shaking hands. That day would be burned into her memory for all eternity.

"What happened?" Audrey demanded. She took a step forward and looked like she wanted to fight something – shield Mika, but this had all happened a long time ago. "What did he do?"

Mika looked at the other witch then and knew in her soul this girl would throw down for her. Why, she didn't know. But Audrey was there for her.

"He raped me in one of the closets. At the time he was betrothed to Selene Kavanagh and they were dating. She was my friend. I didn't know what to do or what to tell her."

Audrey took a step closer. "Did you tell anyone?"

She laughed then. The old pain felt like it was brand new now that she'd cracked open that memory. "I had planned to, but things got complicated. So I didn't. Ever since that night and everything that happened after...I haven't been able to do any basic magic without severe strain."

"But you can do battle magic." Audrey squinted at her. "I'm not going to ask what happened after and why it's complicated. From what I saw in the Witchly News that asshole got what he deserved. But I hope one day you'll be able to tell me."

Mika reached out then and took Audrey's hand in hers – very carefully. "Battle magic...it's fueled by rage and pain and anger. But it's also something I've always had an affinity for."

The silence in the cemetery was somehow comforting.

"I'll work up to telling you," Mika whispered. "But just know...it's going to make you hate me."

"We'll see about that," Audrey said, squeezing her

hand. "Teach me how you throw a spell without an incantation."

Mika smiled slightly and released Audrey's hand. No tingling. She studied her palm and wondered if Audrey was right. Maybe if she could accept what she was capable of, it would no longer control her.

"Yeah, I can teach you." Mika shook out her hand and placed her thumb on her ring finger for the first sigil. "A little practice and you'll definitely make the team."

Audrey smiled. "I'm going to get you on that team too, Mika. You just wait. I'll convince you one of these days. The world needs to see that witches are still warriors."

Her heart clenched painfully at those words.

Mika thought about her grandmother fighting every day to beat the heartbreak that had killed her mother. She thought about Selene fighting against the expectations of marrying some asshole because her parents said so – Kenzie fighting to find a place in a world that didn't want her kind of magic.

She thought about all the women who had testified against Bradley Davis when Mika couldn't.

And Mika decided that witches had always been warriors. Maybe it was time to remind the world of that.

8

Mika looked over at Audrey sitting on the bleachers with a Sumerian book open on her lap. The girl had been true to her word. She was sitting in on this hunter class and no one seemed to mind. If anything most were shocked a witch even cared about hunter classes, let alone two.

"I looked over your transcripts when I saw you were in my class, Ms. Marshall," the instructor said. "But I want to make sure you really want to take this class."

It was hard not to sigh. Mika had thought her transcripts and every test she'd taken to get into the classes she had would make it all easier. But it was like no one trusted her skills or abilities. Every single advanced class wanted her to prove her competency and it was getting frustrating.

"Look, I just want to be another student. I don't want to be singled out. If I can't keep up I'll drop the class." Mika could feel everyone's attention on her, but it would be worse if she had to spar with someone to *prove* she could be in this class.

"I didn't say I thought you couldn't hack it," the instructor stated carefully, tucking his tablet into his back pocket. "I said I wanted to make sure you *want* to be here."

The clarification made her pause and Mika narrowed her eyes. "Would you ask a hunter this?"

Clearly her question made him uncomfortable and he went on as though they'd never had this conversation. "All right, let's begin. Welcome to Swordsmanship for the Hunter. I am Professor Theodore Bartholomew. Yes, that is really my name. Now, I know some of you aren't born hunters, but that's the great thing about our class. You don't have to be born a hunter to be one."

Professor Bartholomew looked at her then and Mika couldn't tell if that was a jab at witches, or if he was trying to include her. She crossed her arms over her chest and glared anyway.

At least the training center was airy and bright. The building was gothic stone just like the rest of the school, but there were more skylights than she'd seen anywhere else so far.

Swords were displayed on one wall, and bleachers took up the opposite wall. Flags hung over the bleachers indicating tournaments that had been won and that kind of thing. Mika had brought her own swords. There was nothing worse than working with an unbalanced, crappy practice sword.

Setting her case on the bleachers near Audrey, Mika

pulled out one of her practice swords – dull but still perfectly balanced and made to fit her hand. She closed the case and pulled at the neck of her shirt.

There was no uniform like there had been in her class in high school. So Mika had worn athletic wear for the winter. It covered her from head to toe – all black of course. And then the leather gloves she wore looked like they were for grip, but it was another layer between her and everyone else. The running shoes she wore would help with speed, but she would have to be careful. Any natural born hunters would be much stronger and faster than her.

The instructor started pairing people up, telling them to grab a practice sword from the wall or to take out their own. Mika glanced at Audrey sitting on the bleachers, not even pretending to read anymore. She gave Mika a thumb's up in encouragement.

"Hey, the prof paired us."

Mika looked up and froze. Did they accept all the guys here based on their beauty or what? She'd never seen so many gorgeous men in her life until she'd walked through the portal to the University of Morgana.

"I'm Lucien." He grinned down at her and Mika almost wanted to grin back, but she was too busy taking in his golden skin, long black hair that brushed his shoulders, and the necklaces around his neck.

Lucien looked like a Korean rock star, but he was also a hunter which meant his shoulders were broad and he was absolutely ripped.

Mika cleared her throat delicately. "Mika. Born hunter?" she asked, getting into position.

That grin of his widened somehow and it was almost vulpine. "Does it matter, witch?"

Well. "No, it doesn't." Mika whipped the sword across her body, reminding her muscles what needed to be done.

They stared at each other while the instructor explained to them how rare it would be to need a sword, but also how some creatures would be easier to fight with one. Then he launched into a bit of history about hunters and swords.

Mika was barely listening. She couldn't take her eyes off Lucien. Something about him set her instincts on edge and she refused to let him out of her sight.

Even Lucien's teeth seemed sharper than a normal person's. "I hope you're as fun to play with as you look, little witch."

Mika gripped her sword tight as she tried to regain control over her temper. "I'm not little," she hissed. It wasn't her fault this guy was so tall. Tall Asian men happened to be one of her weaknesses, but she'd never admit that to anyone.

Lucien whipped his sword as well and then let it fall to his side as he waited for the signal to begin.

That wasn't a good sign. She didn't think Lucien thought she was incapable. Which meant he thought he was really that good. And from what she could see he probably was.

Mika licked her lips and took a deep breath. Relaxing

her grip on her sword she forced her body to go loose. Her weight was balanced and she could move at a moment's notice. But Mika already knew Lucien was going to kick her ass.

Training as a hunter wasn't the same as being one.

The bell chimed and Lucien didn't attack first. Instantly her heart started beating hard enough she felt like everyone could hear it.

Mika hated attacking first – hated it with a passion. But Lucien was a hunter. She knew without a shred of doubt he would wait for her – as long as it took for his prey to make the first move. She was the rabbit and he was the fox.

Was she fast enough to escape him?

If she was a white hare in the snowy landscape…maybe.

Mika calmed her heart with another cleansing breath and looked down. Lucien was stronger than her, but was he faster? She vividly remembered Kenzie telling Selene one of the times she'd been visiting that they had to be faster, because they wouldn't always be stronger.

It was what had convinced Mika that avoiding conflict was a thousand times more effective than bashing her head against a wall.

One step to the right and Lucien shifted his weight. Still she kept her eyes down so he couldn't read her and watched his feet, relying on her peripheral vision. She went completely still, just like a rabbit.

The clash and clang of other swords was loud and

then it faded into nothing as she concentrated – until Lucien's breathing was all she heard.

Then Mika struck.

He blocked it like she'd expected he would, already moving into a parry, but Mika had anticipated that. She was already moving in the opposite direction, nowhere near his sword. Attacking her like he was left his side completely open and she went for it.

But Lucien was *fast* – inhumanly fast. If he wasn't a natural born hunter, he sure as shit wasn't just a human.

His sword came up and met hers and suddenly they were locked together.

"Clever little witch," he whispered. "I like the way you think."

Mika made the mistake of looking up into his eyes. The dark pools were playful and intrigued. Lucien studied her as they both strained against each other.

"You can't hold this for long," he warned her. "What are you going to do little witch?"

"Stop calling me that." Mika stomped on his foot and shoved him away from her at the same time.

Lucien stumbled backward with a laugh. But her breathing room was short lived. He was attacking her without mercy now, faster and faster until it was all she could do to keep up. Then she lost her balance and Mika knew she was going to fall flat on her back.

But his hand shot out and he grabbed her forearm. Mika looked down at the floor that was so close to her face, breathing hard. Glancing up at Lucien, she didn't know what to make of him. He was grinning down at her, sweat on his brow.

"Your name means 'new moon' in Japanese," Lucien murmured, pulling her up slowly. When she was practically pressed against his chest he stared into her eyes like he was looking for something. "But I have a feeling you're more the Native American meaning."

She yanked out of his grip, feeling unnerved for some reason, and yet – insanely curious. "And which one is that?" she asked.

"Intelligent raccoon." Lucien grinned and tilted his head. "You're a smart fighter and scrappy. It's a good strategy against those who are stronger than you."

This had taken a weird turn.

"Why don't you just stick to Mika?" she snapped.

"Everything okay here?" Professor Bartholomew asked.

Suddenly the sounds of clashing swords came back and Mika blinked, taking another step away from Lucien, even though the memory of his touch was like a brand on her arm.

"Everything's fine," Mika said. "Lucien was just showing me how to evade a stronger attacker."

"Seems like you're right on track for this class," Bartholomew agreed. "But you also could do with some extra practice. At this level you should know better than to lock with a stronger opponent."

Clearly.

Lucien just grinned as the instructor walked away, yelling for everyone to start practicing defensive maneuvers. Looked like they were going to end up going through the basics again.

Was this what university was? A general repeat of everything they'd done in high school? When would they get to the new stuff?

Mika sighed and shook out her arm. Blocking and parrying against Lucien wasn't going to be fun.

"Do you have a boyfriend?" Lucien asked, getting into position.

"That's really none of your business," Mika told him, glancing over at Audrey.

Her dorm mate was grinning. That wasn't a good sign.

"I was just making pleasant conversation." Lucien attacked faster than her eyes could easily follow.

Mika just barely blocked him in time. Once again he was pressed up against her and they were breathing the same air. Why did she keep making mistakes with this guy?

"I don't have a girlfriend," Lucien told her. Then he stepped back. "You're distracted. I was very obvious about my attack. Do better next time."

She gritted her teeth and gripped her sword hard enough it practically burned. "I'm not distracted."

Smiling, he watched his sword whip through the air in a fancy little pattern, and then he crouched into position. "So I'm not distracting you with my charm?"

This time when he attacked, Mika was ready. She parried with a complex slither along his sword and managed to disarm him as well. The sword went up into the air and she kicked him—hard.

It wasn't enough to really do damage since he was so much larger and stronger than her, but it did shove him out of the way. Mika caught his sword before he could and aimed both points at his throat.

"Why would you possibly be distracting me?" she asked.

Lucien grinned, hands up in submission.

Mika couldn't help the way her lips twitched into a half smile. She tossed his sword back to him and Lucien deftly caught it. "Again."

9

Audrey sat across from Mika in the library, doing their homework for Intermediate Sumerian. "So, are we going to talk about that hottie in your hunter class?"

"No." Mika finished translating the spell they'd been given and started making a list of ingredients. If the spell went the way it was supposed to, she'd translated it correctly. If it didn't...well, let's just say her Sumerian professor was a 'sink or swim' kind of woman.

Thankfully the spell was simple and Audrey promised to help her with it – turn a seed into a fully mature plant. Helping nature along was natural for witches and didn't take much energy. There was a possibility she might even be able to do it by herself.

Mika was mildly annoyed she had to do magic in a language class. She had been stupidly unprepared. Honestly, she thought she'd be able to get through this whole semester without having to do any actual magic so she would have the time to figure out how to get past her block.

She'd thought that being out of that house and on her own would help. Granted it had only been a few days, but Mika felt like she should have improved more already. Breathing all this fresh, clean, northern air was supposed to help them all focus in a place where the cold grounded them ten months out of twelve.

A five hundred acre island north of New York. It had been wiped from the memories of the humans and hidden for hundreds of years. Hundreds of witches had lived here during the witch hunts – it had been a sanctuary and still was.

Mika could feel it – a calming effect.

"Ignoring me isn't going to keep me from talking about it. He was seriously into you."

"I don't think he was born a hunter," Mika murmured, writing down the correct pronunciation of the incantation.

Audrey's eyes widened and she leaned in closer. "What do you think he is? He definitely doesn't move like a human."

"I'm not sure, but it doesn't really matter. I was just making an observation." Mika looked up and put her pen down, running her finger along the inscription from her father. "Why are we talking about him? I mean the real reason."

Audrey grinned and snatched Mika's notes to look them over. "I think you need to loosen up and a cute boy

– or girl – could really help you out. You need some serious serotonin, Mika."

She sighed and tapped her nails on the table. "Maybe, but that's not why I'm here."

"Yeah, I know why you're here – you're the chick who's taking eight fucking classes. But it can't be all work and no play Mika. That's how we lose our sanity."

"I'm trying to graduate on time."

Audrey set the paper down on the table and gave her a look. "I call bullshit. Your classes are too varied. Sure, it doesn't matter with an undeclared specialty. But I think you're trying to find something you're good at. And the annoying thing is – you're good at everything but actual magic."

They both looked down at the spell, knowing she might not be able to do it even if she'd translated it perfectly.

"You need to get rid of that block and if screwing the brains out of a hot guy helps, then do it." Audrey shrugged and pushed the paper back to Mika.

Mika snorted as she studied her spell one last time. "Everyone here is hot."

"Seriously!" Audrey sat back and looked around at the other students studying. "I thought I was the only one who'd noticed."

Someone sat down right next to Mika – as if there weren't a thousand other seats available in a library so large it had five stories, three aboveground and two below. The library took up almost the *entire* east wing. No doubt there was at least one seat available that wasn't *right next* to her.

Mika looked up, eyebrow raised.

Ethan was leaning against the table with his head propped up on his hand, staring at her.

"Really?" she asked.

"You never said anything about my drawing. I was wondering if you'd even gotten it." Ethan didn't smile but his eyes twinkled. "And I couldn't wait until tomorrow to know what you thought."

Mika gritted her teeth and tried not to think of the paper tucked into her coat pocket. "Your still life is excellent, though I do have a critique." She grabbed her notes and books, shoving them into her bag.

"Really, what is it?" he was almost smiling now.

"Maybe next time stick to the plants. Practice your human anatomy before drawing a portrait." Mika stood and jerked her head at Audrey.

Her dorm mate was too busy watching with wide eyes and grinning like an idiot. But she scrambled to get her stuff together when Mika got up and started walking toward the closest exit.

Why were all these fucking boys practically begging for her attention? Did she have to wear a damn sign that said 'unavailable?'

"Excellent constructive criticism," Ethan called after her, earning a few glares from the other students. "I'll see you in class tomorrow!"

Mika didn't dare speed up, but she didn't dawdle either. "Let's go see if that spell works," she muttered to

Audrey. "I have enough homework to drown a horse and I can't seem to get a moment's peace."

They practically burst out of the library. The second they were in the spacious hall with floor to ceiling windows looking out over the wintry landscape, Audrey was laughing so hard the sound echoed.

"It's not funny." Mika crossed her arms over her chest.

"You should make a game out of this," Audrey said between giggles. "Seriously, make them compete against each other or something. Because sweet thing, you're on everyone's radar."

"Why?" Mika demanded. "I have done everything I can to make it clear I'm *not interested*."

Audrey stopped laughing as they walked through the halls to the dormitories. The silence wasn't heavy or difficult to bear, but Mika was curious what the other witch was thinking. Ever since she'd gotten here Audrey had pushed her and pushed her to leave her comfort bubble.

Part of her was grateful, and part of her just wanted to ask Audrey to let it go. She didn't want to be anyone's project.

"So I've been thinking about it and I've come to two conclusions," Audrey said, holding the door open for her. Freezing cold air blasted them and Mika buttoned up her coat as they headed across the quad to the dorms.

"What have you come up with?" Mika asked, slipping on her gloves and shoving her hands into her pockets. This was bound to be an interesting theory.

"Either you don't realize how gorgeous you are – how enigmatic you can be to the point that everyone just gravitates toward you. Or you're doing all this on purpose to fuck with people."

She glanced sideways at Audrey and glared. "Really? I'm either stupid or bitchy?"

Audrey laughed and linked her arm through Mika's as they slushed through the snow. "I mean when you boil it down to the basics, I guess. But honestly if I thought I could sway you to my team, I'd be trying just as hard as these boys."

That made Mika blush but she slogged on, eyeing their dorm near the tree line. "I don't have the time or energy to be in a relationship and care about someone the way they deserve to be cared about. If you could tell me what exactly I'm doing to encourage people, then I'll stop."

Snow started falling from the sky and they picked up their pace. The sun was going to set soon and it was already freezing.

"It's not anything you're doing," Audrey told her. "You're just...fascinating. Most people are easy to read, and two seconds after talking to them you see they're not really that deep. But you—it's like we're all sucked in by the layers in your eyes and then you open your mouth and it's over. Just seeing you take the classes you do piques everyone's curiosity. Do you know how many people I've had asking me about you and if you're really this broody all the time?"

Audrey laughed again like this was all hilarious and

started running as the snow fell faster. Mika kept up as best she could, but the snow on the ground was deep.

"I'm not broody," Mika protested, pushing open the heavy wooden door to their dorms.

It was gloriously warm and the common room had three fires going. Other students looked up briefly and then went back to studying when they'd satisfied their curiosity.

She still had so much homework to do, but Mika needed a hot chocolate and a scone if she was going to be able to concentrate on the interdimensional physics equations that were due the next day.

"You're extremely broody, but that's just part of your charm." Audrey set down her bag on one of the empty tables near a fire and started taking off her coat, scarf, and gloves. "Do you want snacks?"

Mika did the same and hung up her stuff on the coat tree. "Definitely. I was just thinking I needed hot chocolate."

Audrey grinned. "With brandy. That's my favorite drink."

"No brandy." Mika pulled out her books and sighed. Maybe eight classes were too many.

"Yes, brandy." Audrey disappeared through the door in the back of the common room to the massive kitchen decorated in silver and black that was available to their entire building. Mika could hear her in there clanging pots and pans.

She wouldn't ask. Mika would just drink whatever Audrey put in front of her.

Sitting down at the desk she pulled out the seed her Sumerian professor had given each of them. It was a moonflower seed if she was right – related to the morning glory, but extremely common in a witch's moon garden.

It was toxic if ingested, but otherwise it wasn't harmful.

Getting this to bloom wouldn't be easy, but it was nearly nightfall. That would make it easier. Forcing night-blooming plants to flower during the day was unnecessarily difficult when she could just wait a few hours.

So Mika set that aside to do last and pulled out her Advanced Latin. It would be relatively easy considering it was practically her first language. She'd agreed to tutor Audrey though. For someone who had started their witch studies late in life, the girl was extremely adept.

Audrey had learned languages on the internet while in the psych ward, and studied what she could. Some spells worked and some didn't, but whatever she'd learned since turning eighteen – she'd absorbed it like it was all second nature.

It was really impressive for a witch born into a human family.

"Hot chocolate for my grumpy hottie," Audrey said, setting down a cup with whipped cream on top. "Now, how much homework do you have?"

"Thank you." Mika took a sip and decided not to say anything about the extra kick of alcohol. It did make it taste really good. "Poisons and Swordsmanship don't have any homework. I finished Latin, Runes, and Shifter

Studies. So growing this moonflower, interdimensional physics equations, and then a paper for History of Magic. But I'm ready to help you with Latin first."

"Damn girl, you are way more on top of your homework than I am." Audrey pulled out her Latin and Beginning of Magic books. "I appreciate all your help by the way – with the battle magic and these harder classes."

Mika shrugged. "My high school was solely for paranormals. I have a bit of a head start. And I don't mind helping you. You deserve it."

They both sipped on the hot chocolate and Audrey grinned, pushing the plate of scones toward her. "You know it's not all homework and classes here right?"

She didn't like the sound of that. "We have to make this moonflower bloom once the sun completely sets."

"Yes, I know. But I was invited to a party Friday night. You should come."

Mika tapped her nails on the walnut table and tried not to feel annoyed. "Tryouts are on Saturday."

Audrey's grin widened. "We should go to this hunter party over at Wolfsbane House."

"I thought you wanted to make the team," Mika snapped, setting her mug down harder than necessary.

"Oh, I'm going to make the team," Audrey said with a smirk. "But I think we should celebrate your first week. We'll be home before the sun rises – I promise."

Mika didn't want to go. She thought this was a terrible idea and definitely not the way to stay off everyone's radar. Not to mention there would probably be dancing and drinking and Fates knew what else –

magic probably, knowing how witches liked to show off for the hunters.

"Please Mika?" Audrey asked. "I won't bother you about boys again as long as you do fun things with me. You need to get out of your head."

She sipped the spiked drink and considered Audrey's request. Doing it her way certainly hadn't helped remove her block. Maybe the other witch was right and just letting go would help. "Fine, I'll go to this party, but if you don't make the team I don't have to go to another party the entire semester."

"Oh, you drive a hard bargain." But Audrey's eyes were twinkling. "You've got a deal, babe."

Audrey stuck her hand out so they could shake on it. Mika hesitated. But she took a deep breath and shook the other witch's hand once. "Now, let's translate this set of spells."

"Now that we've covered most of the average poisonous plants and flowers, we're going to move onto the ones that are a bit rarer," Professor Hayes was saying.

But Mika wasn't paying attention. She'd learned all this before she was ten. There were other plants on the syllabus that she was more interested in – the deadliest human plants, witch plants that didn't exist in the human world, and the hybrids.

Everything up to midterms she could do in her sleep.

"Why are you even taking this class?" Ethan asked under his breath.

Mika didn't bother to reply. She just stared at the plants in the greenhouse with her chin propped up on her hand. Maybe she should have taken more herbology classes. The greenhouse was by far her favorite place and it calmed her in ways she didn't understand.

She and Audrey had gotten up early to train some

more in the battle magic, and then the rules of the dodgeball itself. It was both complex, and yet not. Mika sighed and wished she hadn't had to drop out of the team back in high school – but after what had happened it was the best thing for her to do.

For everyone's sake.

"You're what, a freshman?" Ethan asked. "You must be some kind of genius. This is a notoriously hard class to get into."

She ignored him. After the library incident the day before Mika had decided she needed to be more obvious with her lack of interest – maybe these university boys really were that dense and needed some help getting a clue.

"But from what I can tell you could test out of this class if you wanted to as well. A deadly witch is difficult to resist – something about a woman who could kill me is so sexy."

Finally she looked away from the *Nepenthes attenboroughii* – the Attenborough's pitcher plant that was one of the rarest carnivorous plants on earth – and turned her gaze to Ethan.

Mika studied him like she would a particularly difficult interdimensional physics problem.

It wasn't that he wasn't attractive. Ethan had this whole tall as a tree, super muscular 'I built my own tiny home' hipster thing going on that made her knees weak – it was part of the reason she avoided looking at him whenever possible. But they had an entire semester of this class together as lab partners.

She couldn't ignore him the whole time – that wouldn't help either of them pass.

Something about the way he looked at her was what made Mika so uncomfortable. It wasn't like Lucien. Lucien was hunting her and he was exactly what he appeared to be – and yet…not.

Ethan though, Ethan wanted to get to know her in a way she just wasn't ready for. Mika knew the power this kind of guy could have over her. It would be nothing for him to make her fall in love with him – for her to do anything for him.

And Mika didn't trust herself.

So she had to keep an arm's length away from everyone – just in case.

Just until she could figure her shit out.

"Do you really have a death wish?" she asked.

Ethan wasn't smiling anymore. He was studying her like he wanted to find out exactly why she hurt so much, so he could fix it. "Sometimes I do. I'm a product of my generation after all."

Maybe he was the perfect guy for her after all.

Mika narrowed her eyes. "What exactly is it that you want from me?"

"I know pain when I see it," he murmured, taking her free hand in his. Mika was so shocked by his forwardness that she let him, unable to look away from his large thumb rubbing over one of her silver rings until it shone. She should have put on her gloves. "I know we don't know each other at all, but let me help you shoulder it. I've felt like I was drowning before and all I wanted was for someone to reach out and give me a hand. I'm not trying to save you Mika – but I don't want to watch you drown either."

Her palm started to tingle and Mika panicked. She yanked her hand out of his so hard she nearly fell off her stool. "You don't know anything about me," she gasped, grabbing onto the worktable so she didn't fall.

The room was suddenly quiet and too many people were looking at them.

"Ms. Marshall?" the professor asked carefully – like Mika might just explode.

The tingling got worse and Mika looked at the professor, and then Ethan and just—ran.

She burst through the doors of the poison garden and ran straight for the spiral staircase.

There shouldn't be any classes on the top floor – it would give her the time and space and silence she needed to get shit back under control.

Her boots pounded on the metal but all she could hear was the ringing in her ears and the burning sensation on her palms. Mika ran through the main floor to the room in the back made for plants that required humidity so high her coveralls were soaked the second she opened the door.

It closed firmly behind her and she whirled around to find the trees reaching for the top of the conservatory – reaching for the sun that was hiding behind the clouds as more snow fell. It was starting to pile up and then melt thanks to the heat inside this room – it took only seconds for it to freeze again, creating an extra layer that made the glass look warped.

She took in a deep breath of the warm, humid air, and then another – shaking out her hands to try and get the tingling to stop. But Mika had never learned how to control this. It wasn't something other witches could do – there was no one to ask for help.

"Mika?"

She whipped around and put a hand out. "Get away from me!"

Ethan took a step forward instead of back. "Let me help you."

"You've no idea what you're talking about," she whispered, shoving her hands into her pockets so he couldn't touch her skin.

"You're right," Ethan said, taking another step forward. "I have no idea what I'm talking about – so please, explain it to me."

Three years of this shit and Mika was so tired. Her shoulders slumped. She wanted to trust someone, but she didn't trust *anyone* – especially not with this. "I can't."

"Nothing can be that bad," he murmured, taking that last step. Ethan was so close she could *feel* his magic.

Mika looked up and searched his eyes. "It can and it is."

"When I was sixteen I nearly electrocuted my father to death," Ethan told her quietly, eyes narrowed as he searched her face. "My magic had fully matured and I had thought my specialty was growing things, but I was wrong."

He held out his hand and the moisture in the air started to condense, forming tiny storm clouds. Those clouds crackled and thundered. Then rain began to pour into the palm of his hand.

"A storm witch," Mika whispered, feeling her heart rate decrease as she focused on the beauty in the palm of his hands.

"All magic is dangerous – even something like this that is considered to be beneficial. I help plants grow and give them the water they need. But there is a cost." Ethan grimaced as lightning struck the palm of his hand. He shook out his hands with a whispered word and the storm disappeared.

"I nearly killed my father that night," Ethan told her. "His heart stopped and we rushed him to the hospital. I spent the entire night thinking I'd killed him."

Mika took a deep, calming breath and realized then that his eyes weren't blue or green, but a stormy grey. The tingle started to dissipate and the fear began to recede. "But he lived?"

Ethan nodded, watching her closely. "He made a full recovery, but it took a while for me to conjure a storm with confidence. Fear only holds us back – it only makes the magic more dangerous and unpredictable and volatile. After a lot of practice, I know I'll never accidentally hurt someone again – even when provoked. It's mine to control – to use if I wish."

Their magic wasn't the same, but he understood. Mika let him gently take her wrist and pull it out of her pocket. It made her heart start pounding again, but the tingling was gone now. It wasn't the fear making her react this way this time – but his touch.

She didn't dare blink as Ethan turned her wrist so that her hand was facing palm up, fingers curled inward.

Ethan traced a sigil for peace in her palm and then closed her fingers over the glowing mark. "I don't think you have storm magic, but I can promise you whatever it is you do have, it won't scare me away."

Those words nearly broke her resolve. Mika took in a shuddering breath and held her palm against her chest, wanting that small bit of peace for as long as she could hold it. "I'm less worried about it scaring you than I am about it killing you."

It was more than she'd ever admitted to anyone. Not even Claire really knew – Claire only knew that one day she'd come home crying and covered in blood and ranting about a tonic to ward against pregnancy. Since that day everything had changed, but her sister never said anything – she'd never pried or asked.

Mika had thought it a small mercy, something to be grateful for. But with Ethan towering over her, just a breath away, practically demanding she let him help shoulder her burden...Mika wondered if maybe this kind of friendship – this kind of love was what she really needed.

Tough love – no room for bullshit and lies.

Audrey had it, and now here was someone else asking —no, practically demanding to let him help her.

Ethan wiped away the single tear that fell down her

cheek, but he didn't smile and his touch didn't linger. "Want to see something cool?"

She nodded, glad he didn't ask for details. Instead he drew a few runes in the air and whispered a few words in Sumerian.

Clouds began to form above them and suddenly rain started pouring down on them like a monsoon on the plants. The flowers opened up to drink the water like grateful creatures in the deep desert.

Mika couldn't help but smile, taking her other hand out of her pocket and holding it up to catch the rain completely soaked with her hair plastered to her face. "This is beautiful," she murmured. "Thank you."

Ethan said nothing, he just studied her.

It made her breath catch, but Mika kept her eyes on the clouds inside the greenhouse, enjoying the water her skin absorbed just like the plants did – she never would have thought she would miss the rain.

Then he reached out and wiped a drop of that rain from her bottom lip.

Mika froze—the *world* froze as her entire being focused on that one simple touch.

"I've never met anyone like you before," Ethan admitted, stepping closer. "I have to say...I'm a little obsessed."

It should have been creepy, but the way he said it – it sounded more like he was worshipping a goddess than stalking someone that only existed in his head.

Mika didn't try to pull away when he placed one hand on her lower back and pulled her forward. Her open hand rested on his chest like it was the most natural thing in the world. She should push him away, go back to class, but Mika's lips parted as she looked up into those stormy eyes.

Then she looked down at those lips that begged to be kissed.

Ethan didn't hesitate. He bent down and gently pressed his lips to hers in the most undemanding way. Every thought in Mika's head disappeared and then the rain stopped. But it didn't just stop – it froze into place. She pulled back and looked around, some of the drops seemed to go back up into his clouds and others hung in the air like diamonds.

"You're smiling," Ethan whispered. "I never thought I'd get to see you smile."

Mika looked back at him and she couldn't decipher the look on his face, but it washed away every single word of caution whispering in the back of her mind. She grabbed the back of his neck and pulled him down for a kiss – practically starved for touch, for affection.

Three years of self-imposed isolation and Ethan had somehow managed to break through her walls of iron.

The taste of him was addicting, like freedom. Mika couldn't get enough. She pressed her whole body against his and Ethan gripped her hips hard, groaning when she slipped her tongue inside his mouth.

She pulled back to search his eyes, to see what he was thinking.

But Ethan's eyes were glazed over and his skin was pale.

Mika snatched her hand back and saw it was covered in blood.

Her scream nearly shattered the windows as power exploded from her body with the force of her panic. They continued to rattle as she screamed for help – as she caught Ethan before he fell to the ground, careful not to touch him with her bare skin.

Mika *screamed* as blood poured from him – no visible wounds.

Footsteps pounded and she tried not to remember what had happened three years ago, but it was like history was repeating itself and the Fates were forcing her to relive her worst nightmare.

Mika let them take Ethan. Healing witches tried to do what they could but he was rushed to the infirmary and then she was alone, sitting in a pool of someone else's blood, just like the last time.

S he didn't remember how she got to the infirmary, but someone must have taken her there. Mika vaguely remembered the healers asking her questions and she had to say she didn't know what happened – because she really didn't.

Mika didn't know what exactly her magic was doing when she touched someone while her hands tingled. All she knew was there was suddenly blood everywhere and whoever had skin to skin contact with her was dead.

By some small miracle she hadn't killed Ethan, but he was ghostly pale as he lay in his infirmary bed. Mika sat beside him with her gloves back on her hands, not daring to touch him even then.

Fates, this was exactly why she'd wanted people to leave her alone. It was the only way until she could figure out what the *fuck* her magic was trying to do.

"Ms. Marshall, from what we can tell it looks like there was some kind of charm that went off," the head healer told her, kneeling down in front of her so their faces were level and Mika was forced to focus on her. "He bled from his pores. Blood magic charms aren't forbidden, but they are very dangerous. Do you know where he might have gotten it?"

The ringing in her ears was too loud. Mika couldn't think. She couldn't form thoughts.

Blood magic?

Why had that never fucking occurred to her?

Oh, right.

Because no one had blood magic as a specialty.

Even necromancy was considered taboo. So if there *were* blood witches out there...

Mika dropped her head in her hands and took deep breaths to keep from fainting.

"Hey, he's going to be okay," the healer reassured her. "We're giving him a blood transfusion now. A few hours and he'll be back to normal."

Someone was going to ask her a lot of very uncomfortable questions unless Ethan covered for her, but why would he do that?

She'd nearly killed him.

Her hands shook and tears pricked her eyes. Mika couldn't focus on anything and she wasn't feeling very stable, but she had to be there with him. She had to sit by his side until he woke. This was all her fault after all.

"Mika!"

She should have been more insistent and told him to back off. Mika shouldn't have let a little bit of pretty magic soften her heart. All of this could have been prevented if she hadn't been so weak.

"Mika, holy shit. Are you okay? I heard there was a nasty blood magic charm and..." Audrey trailed off when she knelt down in front of Mika. "Well, fuck. Come here."

Her dorm mate lifted her up and off the chair. Mika was still in shock. She couldn't have resisted even if she'd tried.

"Please don't touch me," she whispered. When Audrey started to look pissed Mika swallowed hard. She had to tell someone. "Don't touch my skin."

Sudden understanding dawned on Audrey's face.

"Fuck, fuck, fuck, fuck, *fuck*. Come with me."

"I can't leave him." After what she'd done, she couldn't just abandon Ethan.

"He's going to live," Audrey hissed. "Which might not be the case next time. So come with me *now*."

Mika stumbled after the other witch, praying to the Fates that Audrey might know of a way to lock her magic up forever so she couldn't hurt anyone. Maybe she should ask Takahashi to strip her of her powers. Or better yet, Kenzie.

It would tear apart the very thing that made her who she was – that connection to the universe and the growing things would be severed in a way she couldn't comprehend, but maybe it would be for the best.

Audrey didn't say anything until they were out of the infirmary wing and even then she was just muttering nonsense as she pulled Mika through the school.

And she let her.

Mika had no sense of purpose or will at the moment. All she could do was hold onto the magic that wanted to burst from her skin. She'd nearly shattered the glass in the greenhouse. What would happen if she lost control again?

Would she go off like a bomb – killing anyone in a ten foot radius of her?

"Here I thought you were just like, good at growing man-eating plants. If I'd known it was literally something that could kill people with a touch I would have pushed you harder. But Mika – battle magic doesn't really translate to *blood magic*," she hissed under her breath.

Audrey opened a random classroom door and checked to make sure it was empty before dragging Mika into it. She was still so out of her mind Mika didn't bother resisting. If someone had to know – Audrey was the best person.

The girl hadn't grown up with witches. She didn't hold the same stigma against certain magics as everyone else did.

A few quick words from Audrey and the room was sealed. No one could overhear their conversation.

"What happened?" Audrey demanded. "The healers think it was a *blood magic* charm Mika."

She collapsed into one of the chairs and looked up at the girl who had basically adopted her as her own. Audrey's dark brown hair with its reddish tint was back in a ponytail today, but her usual pleasant expression was stern as she crossed her arms over her chest to glare at Mika.

"Are you mad because I almost killed someone, or because I didn't tell you?" Mika's voice was so quiet it didn't even echo in the wide open space.

Audrey huffed then and her arms dropped to her side. "I'm not mad. I'm annoyed someone so smart is being such an idiot."

Mika didn't know what to make of that so she shrugged and rested her arms on the desk in front of her, crossing them like she had as a child so they formed a pillow for her head. Laying down she took a deep breath and decided to tell Audrey everything.

"After Bradley Davis...raped me three years ago, I ran. I ran and ran back to my house," she whispered. "I'm still disappointed he wasn't the one I killed."

Audrey's face paled at that.

"I ran into some guy – a human. He was asking me if I was all right and trying to get me to go in the car with him so he could take me home." The blackboard down near the podium still had scribbles from the last class, but Mika couldn't make them out. Based on the images framed on the wall though she'd bet this was a healing classroom.

The other witch didn't say a word but she sat in the chair next to Mika and waited.

Mika slid her gaze to Audrey's. "I was out of my mind, in pain and feeling betrayed. This human was pulling on me and trying to force me into a car. I don't think he was trying to hurt me – I really do think he was trying to help which makes all this so much worse."

The silence was deafening as she remembered how the blood felt like rain if she didn't look too closely. All she could hear was the roar of water in her head.

"I didn't even touch him," Mika whispered. "He grabbed my bare arm and I freaked."

The water had bowed outwards then, like she'd created an invisible shield around them and the rain ran down that sphere instead of continuing its natural path.

"At first nothing happened, but then he got so pale and that's when he let go of me." Mika looked away from Audrey, feeling that shame and fear all over again. "He started shaking first. Then blood poured out of his eyes and nose and mouth and ears. I grabbed onto him so he didn't fall into the street. When my hand touched his skin...that's when blood started oozing out of his pores."

Mika closed her eyes, wishing she could burn the memory of all that blood – covering her and staining her white Beltane dress until it was red all over...

"I called 911 and left an anonymous tip and then— and then I ran all the way home. Claire never asked whose blood was all over me or why I wanted a tonic to prevent pregnancy. She just burned my dress and got me cleaned up. Then she made me that tonic and put me to bed. She stayed with me all night."

She could feel Audrey's gaze like a stone on her back. Mika sighed and turned her head to look at her dorm mate. "I haven't been able to do basic magic since then – nothing that isn't my *specialty*," she spat.

Audrey drummed her fingers on the desk. "It still doesn't make sense. Battle magic has nothing to do with blood magic and yet, you can do that just fine."

Mika shrugged. "Both are offensive and can kill people."

"And there are a ton of blood magic spells that have nothing to do with harming people," Audrey went on.

"I don't pretend to understand it," Mika muttered, wishing she could go to sleep and wake up and realize this was all a bad dream. "I just want to get rid of it."

A hand slapped the desk right next to her face, hard. "Snap out of it, Mika. Accidents happen, but doing nothing is going to turn you into a real murderer if you don't figure out how to control this."

Mika sat up then and glared. "It would be better if my High Priestess just stripped me of my powers. Then there wouldn't be any more accidents while I try to figure out a deadly magic."

"Don't be stupid. Giving up is not the answer," Audrey snapped. She grabbed Mika's jacket and shook her. "That would be like cutting off both your legs because sometimes you fall. You are helping me, now let me help you."

Mika stared at this girl who was somehow exactly what she needed. And her resolve shattered just like it had with Ethan. Tears streamed down her face and she just...crumbled. Audrey caught her and held on – Mika gripped the other girl tight, still careful of her skin, but... Audrey had seen what she could do and still wasn't afraid of her.

"I'm disappointed in your sister," Audrey muttered into her hair, stroking Mika's back. "She should have asked more questions. Someone should have asked why you couldn't do magic anymore."

Mika had held onto that very same disappointment until it had turned to an ever-burning rage at her family. Finding out her father and brother had betrayed her had just been the icing on the cake.

"To be fair she was only home for a few days. Claire was living here at the university when it all happened." Mika knew her sister had said something to their mother, but there was only so much she could do from so far away – and Mika hadn't trusted anyone in her family. High society witches aren't the kindest creatures.

"It doesn't matter anymore," Audrey murmured. "We'll figure this out. I promise."

She didn't ask how or why. Mika could just feel it. Audrey would help her sort things out – she didn't have to be alone in this struggle anymore.

She took in a shuddering breath and thanked the Fates for sending her Audrey. It actually felt possible with this girl on her side.

Mika stared at the section in the library on blood magic. Audrey was next to her and they both just stood there, taking it in. Then Audrey took a step closer to her and laced her fingers through Mika's gloved ones.

"I had no idea books could be so creepy."

"Wait until you see demon books," Mika whispered. "Some of them are sentient."

"Okaaaaay, definitely have no plans to do that any time soon." Audrey practically pressed into the entire left side of Mika's body. "Why does this area feel so creeeeeeeeeepy?"

"Blood magic is considered a dark magic," Mika whispered. "Like necromancy, and even battle magic. Witches weren't always neutral, but since we declared ourselves such these kinds of magics have been...avoided."

Mika could do this. She took one step over the

invisible line into the vast section of the library dedicated to blood magic.

A chill ran down her spine. Some of these books were evil. But not all blood magic had to be evil right?

"Maybe this was a bad idea," Mika whispered.

"Oh, most definitely," Audrey agreed, but she took another step forward. "But I can't think of any other way to get the information we need. It's not like there's a blood witch just...around."

"I'm not even sure that's a thing," Mika said, taking another step forward. "I've never heard of blood witches."

"Well, no one knew void witches were a thing until there was one," Audrey told her. "I heard Kenzie has a demon training her. Maybe we should ask him."

"Eisheth?" Mika would never forget that demon in her life – not when he had crashed multiple coven meetings and the High Priestess hadn't said a word. "I don't think that's a good idea."

"Why not?" Audrey peered closer at one of the books on the shelf. "He's older than dirt. I'm pretty sure if anyone knows about blood witches, he would."

"I'm not summoning a goddamn demon," Mika hissed.

Audrey rolled her eyes and gave Mika a look like she was being particularly dumb today. "No duh. But you know Kenzie. Ask her to ask him."

Well, that was actually not a bad idea.

"Let's see what we can find here first." Mika reached out for one of the books, gripping Audrey tight with her other hand.

Her gloves kept her skin from touching the least awful-looking book. The spine didn't have a title and neither did the front.

"Oh gross, this one is bound in human skin," Audrey said, shoving a book back onto the shelf. She rubbed her hand on her coat and pulled out her gloves. "This is so not what I had planned for today."

"As soon as Ethan is out of the infirmary I'll keep training you," Mika promised, flipping open the book. "Tryouts are in two days."

"I'm honestly surprised you agreed to skip your classes today."

Mika shrugged. She could do most everything in her classes already. A few days of extra homework and her attendance wouldn't even matter. "You didn't have to do this with me."

"I told you I would help you," Audrey murmured, peering over her shoulder. "Skipping classes is just a bonus."

"This one might actually be helpful." Mika flipped another page. "I mean, it's in Classical Nahuatl which is not really something I've studied much."

Audrey gave her a look.

"Aztecs," Mika explained. "This is in their language."

Understanding dawned on Audrey's face. "That makes so much sense. But wouldn't there just be a lot of information on blood sacrifices?"

Mika flipped through a few more pages, skimming over the ones with detailed illustrations as quickly as she could. "Well yeah, but it's not inherently evil. They sacrificed animals mostly. Like the Vikings. I should look for some books by them too."

"Excellent start," a cultured voice said from directly behind them.

Mika jumped and whipped around as her heart leapt into her throat. The book fell and that demon caught it before it hit the ground.

Eisheth just grinned at her and Audrey as he handed the book back.

No one said anything and Mika couldn't bring herself to take the book from the demon.

"What are you doing here?" she asked instead.

"I heard whispers of my name and it made me curious." He set the book on the nearest table and then slipped his hands into his pockets. The demon looked her up and down. "Well, this has certainly been the most exciting decade in a long time. I'd say it was my birthday but I don't actually know when that is."

Then the demon looked to Audrey.

Mika took a step in front of her dorm mate. She didn't know much about this demon other than he was training Kenzie, but she didn't really trust demons.

Eisheth grinned at her. "Protective. And with the power to back it up." He tilted his head at her and that grin widened. "Even with a block. How fascinating."

At this point she should say something, but Mika had no idea how to deal with a demon who hadn't been summoned. She was kicking herself for saying his name out loud. It was one of those things they were taught very early and she'd been stupid enough to do it anyway.

Don't use a demon's name if you don't want to bring their attention to you.

A snap of the demon's fingers and about ten books slid out slightly from the blood magic shelves. "Start with those." Another snap and a business card appeared out of smoke in his hand. Eisheth handed it over to her with a little flourish. "I've been spending so much time on this plane I decided to get my own business cards made. If you need anything, you're allowed to call, Mika Morganna Gabrielle Marshall."

The demon winked and then disappeared into thin air. There was no *pop* or smoke or anything. He was just...gone.

"What. The. Fuck," Audrey whispered. "Oh my god. Let me see that." The other witch snatched the card out of her hand and peered at it like it was going to disappear just like the demon.

Mika was too shocked to move. "He knew my middle name," she muttered. "How the hell did he know that? We keep our second middle names out of public record for a reason."

"What?" Audrey frowned up at her. "What are you talking about?"

She blinked and focused on the other witch. "Born witches don't put their second middle names on birth certificates or any documents so demons can't know our true names. But *that* demon knows mine."

"Morganna," Audrey snorted. "Of course. Are you related to her?"

"Shh!" Mika hissed. "You're the only soul on this

planet who knows that name other than my sister. Now keep it to yourself and never say it out loud again."

Audrey studied her and then nodded. "So I'm fucked then. My whole name is out there for the entire world to Google."

"No, we'll just give you a second middle name on the next new moon," Mika told her, snatching the business card back and tucking it into her coat pocket right next to the drawing Ethan had done for her. "Let's grab these and get them back to our room. I want to get back to the infirmary before he wakes up."

Audrey started grabbing the books that were sticking out on her side. "I don't think he'll tattle on you. That boy is obsessed."

Mika snorted and started grabbing the ones on her side. "That's literally what he said right before I almost killed him."

With each book she felt less and less afraid. Mika was no longer alone. She had a demon on her side – whether she wanted him or not. And she had Audrey. She shook her head and smiled ruefully. The universe wasn't taking her shit anymore.

Everyone who had offered to help her hadn't really given her a choice – and maybe that's what she needed. Pushy friends to get her to see what was right in front of her face.

Mika couldn't ignore her problems anymore. It hadn't worked for the last three years.

And now it was time to try something new.

Ethan was still unconscious, but his coloring was much better. Mika still didn't dare touch him.

She had no idea what he was thinking or feeling about what had happened.

Any minute now he would open his eyes.

The healers had said the pain of a blood magic charm was excruciating and that he had to mentally recover as well. Mika felt terrible.

But she had warned him.

No one had wanted to believe her.

It was part of the reason she hadn't said anything to anyone. 'Mika, you're overreacting.' 'Mika, it can't be that bad.' 'Mika, that doesn't justify what you did.'

No one had known about that night but Brad and now the asshole was dead, thank the Fates. Mika no longer had to look over her shoulder when she was in the coven building. She no longer had to wonder if he would do it again.

Had she known he was a serial rapist she would have said something, but she'd been terrified. What he'd done had left ripples in her life she'd shoved down in the deep dark recesses of her mind.

Her sister had to ask their mother for the tonic and that had spread through her family like wildfire. Mika was no longer a virgin.

Their mother hadn't known about the blood covered dress, but it wouldn't have made a difference.

The transgression had been reported and Mika's engagement to her boyfriend – that had been agreed on when she'd turned three – had been disintegrated. The contract had required she be a virgin – some stupid rule only high society witches still followed from the last century.

It was there for a reason though – for their protection.

A virgin witch had to be protected until her magic fully matured. A broken witch was useless, or worse – dangerous and unpredictable. It forced every male to protect the females or risk losing them.

Which made her wonder, had Brad done it on purpose? Had he done it to make her virtually powerless?

The thought made her sick and Mika almost vomited right then and there. She put her hand on her stomach and took deep breaths to calm down. The last thing she needed was to be admitted to the infirmary too.

Mika had thought the disintegration of her engagement – her betrothal – had been for the best though. The pain of breaking up with her boyfriend hadn't been easy. Fates, she'd loved that boy with her entire heart and soul.

But it was safer for him this way. She didn't have to worry about hurting him.

Sometimes she wondered what her life would have been like had she told her family the truth. But Mika knew the reality, the rape would have been buried as shameful and they would have sent her away to get the block removed – the equivalent of a psych ward for witches.

The last three years had been lonely, but at least she'd been free.

Would she beg Matthew to take her back if she could get control of her magic again?

Mika looked up at Ethan and decided that the Mika who had loved that boy didn't exist anymore. He would always have a place in her heart and she remembered him fondly, but Matthew wasn't the kind of guy who could handle blood magic.

He was too sweet and gentle.

And she...she was not.

It was late and dark. The infirmary was empty, beds along the walls like in the old hospitals. Only curtains separated them from each other, but Ethan was the only one there at the moment so she could see the entire length of the infirmary on this floor.

The floor above was where the private offices for the doctors and healers were. There were private exam rooms there as well. This floor was like an ER rather than somewhere a patient would be admitted.

She studied Ethan and the way his hair curled over his forehead. Mika wished she had the guts and control to brush it back without worrying if she'd make him worse.

Taking another deep breath she let it out slowly and took out one of the books the demon had been so nice to suggest. She had a lot of reading to do based on the stack of books currently sitting on her nightstand.

"Mika?"

She looked up to see Ethan peering at her in confusion. The small sphere of warm light that encased them in the darkness made his brown hair appear gilded and his coloring looked a thousand times better than before.

"How are you feeling?" she asked. Her voice was barely above a whisper in the heavy silence of the infirmary.

"What are we doing here?" he asked. Ethan sat up in the bed and looked around like the answers to all his questions were hiding in the dark.

"What do you remember?" Mika closed her book and handed him a glass that the nurse had told her to give him when he woke. "Drink all of this. It will make you feel better."

"We were in the greenhouse and I made you a storm." He frowned then and sipped the tonic. "Then I kissed you." Ethan gave her a wink and his eyes sparkled at her. "And you kissed me back. After that I don't remember."

Mika watched him down the tonic and she took the

glass from him when he was finished. Ethan took her hand in his before she could move away and studied the elbow-length gloves she wore – inside. Mika snatched her hand back and placed the glass carefully on the nightstand.

"I nearly killed you," she told him quietly.

Touching Audrey with the gloves on was fine. Nothing happened. But Ethan made her entire body stand up and pay attention. She didn't trust the gloves to keep her magic from reaching out for him again even if she understood why.

He was gorgeous and entrancing.

"How the hell did you nearly kill me?" Ethan asked, staring at her in disbelief. He looked down at her gloved hands again and frowned. "Why are you wearing those Mika?"

She glanced around nervously. "Can you do a silencing spell?"

Ethan drew a sigil in the air and then spoke the word to seal a small bubble around them the size of the light. She looked up and admired the way it sparkled.

"Why can't you do the spell?" he asked.

Mika flexed her fingers and decided to tell him everything. He deserved the truth after what she'd done to him. So Mika told him in whispered words what had happened to her as briefly as she could and why she couldn't do basic magic. His eyes grew wider as she explained but he didn't look disgusted or worse – frightened.

At this point, Mika didn't think she could handle Ethan being afraid of her. He was one of the ones who'd asked to help her. Now that she knew what it felt like to share the secret...she didn't want him to abandon her.

"It didn't occur to me my affinity was blood magic until the healer mentioned it looked like you were hit with a blood magic charm," she whispered, looking down at her hands. "I knew I shouldn't have touched you."

His large hand took hers and Mika stared at it in wonder and disbelief. She'd nearly killed him and still he wanted to risk it.

"I should have listened to you," Ethan admitted. "But to be fair, I didn't think sucking blood out of my body through my pores was something you could do with a simple touch." The idiot even laughed at that. "What does it say about me that I find you even sexier now?"

Mika couldn't help her snort of laughter. "It says you're deranged and stupid."

Ethan tugged her forward and out of her chair. Then he scooted over and patted the spot next to him. "You're covered in clothes. Just sit next to me. I promise I won't kiss you. For now."

Her breathing hitched and Mika stared down at this guy who was willing to risk it all again just to be close to her. "Why?"

"Because Mika, I think you're a goddess – like Adrestia. Now, sit down and cuddle me already."

She slid into the bed next to him carefully, pulling up her scarf so it covered her neck, chest, and most of her face. Only the skin around her eyes and forehead was exposed. "Who is Adrestia?"

Ethan put his arm around her shoulders and tucked her into his side, careful not to touch her face. His fingers were still laced in hers and Mika studied their hands, wondering if she would ever be able to do this without all these layers between them.

"She is the daughter of Ares and Aphrodite," Ethan told her, running his thumb over her shoulder in a soothing pattern. "She would go into war with Ares – 'she who none can escape.' The goddess of revenge and retribution – she is the equilibrium, the balance between good and evil, and so beautiful that gods and titans fought over her."

Mika didn't know what to say to that. Ethan was a never-ending surprise and he was exactly the kind of guy she knew he'd be – one who would easily make her fall head over heels in love with him if she wasn't careful.

"Just because you have an affinity for blood magic – it doesn't make you evil," Ethan whispered. He spoke a single word and the bubble of silence disappeared. "You too can be a daughter of war and love."

"Your poetic ass is trying too hard," she whispered back.

Ethan laughed and kissed her hair. "I also like to live dangerously."

Mika squeezed his hand and sighed, the fear of him rejecting her after he found out the truth finally completely dissipated. "Thank you for this."

"Anytime." Then Ethan took her hand and kissed her

gloved knuckles. "Get back to your room and get some sleep. I'll see you around."

She slid off the bed and wrapped her coat tighter around herself. Mika gave Ethan a nod and then turned to leave.

These friends of hers were dangerous. They gave her hope.

Friday was the best day of the week. It was the beginning of a three day weekend and Mika didn't care that it was every week.

After everything that had happened…it was easily one of the worst and best first weeks she could remember.

Nearly managed to kill a guy she was attracted to – *so* Mika.

Then shoved her foot in her mouth at least a dozen times.

Nearly killed her dorm mate and new friend with the only magic she was capable of doing – par for the course, Mika.

And then met the infamous Eisheth who seemed to have a newfound interest in her. As flattering as some might consider that, Mika wasn't thrilled.

Demons were a pain in the ass.

She cracked an eye open and surveyed her room to make sure her thoughts hadn't conjured him. Mika wouldn't put it past the demon to be silently watching her sleep with his hip leaning against her desk, hands in his pockets.

But she was alone in the room, thank the Fates.

Audrey's bed was empty and made. Mika checked her watch and groaned. It was nearly eleven in the morning and she had way too much to do for the few hours left of daylight.

Friday was the only day of the week she didn't have to attend a class. It was the day she'd dedicated to finishing all her homework so she could actually enjoy the weekend. Mika had to finish her own homework *and then* tutor Audrey.

It was definitely going to be a long day.

And to top it all off Audrey was still holding her to that deal they'd made. Apparently most of the student body had been invited to the hunters' 'First Week Back' party and it was legendary. They did it every year, or so she heard.

Even Claire had told her she should go, telling her how awesome the last one she'd attended had been.

Mika had finally made time to call home. Claire was stressed and the strain was starting to wear on her, Mika could tell by the tightness in her sister's voice. But there wasn't much she could do to help.

Her grandmother was still alive; thank the Fates, Artemis, Hecate...whoever was listening. But her condition hadn't changed. Mika just tried to take comfort from the fact that her grandmother hadn't worsened since she left. She'd been worried the extra absence would be the straw that broke the camel's back.

But Mika doubted her grandmother had even realized she'd left – that's how out of it she was.

"Breakfast! Eat up! We have a lot of work to do today and you need the energy."

Mika peered over her quilt at her roommate. The blanket was pulled all the way up to her eyes. "I don't see any food."

"It's in the kitchen dummy. I've been slaving away to thank you for training me and tutoring me."

Audrey was a morning person. It was terrible.

"How long have you been awake?" Mika pulled the blanket over her head and snuggled deeper into the covers. It was snowing again outside and while it was beautiful, it was also cold. These old buildings could be drafty even with the warming spells and the fireplaces.

"Only a few hours. I went for a run, made a smoothie, checked on you, and then started cooking. Ready to get through some of these books Eish—that demon suggested?"

"You better pray he doesn't come to check in on us," Mika grumbled, throwing the covers off.

Audrey shrugged and inspected her nails. How she looked so cute in those oversized sweaters was beyond Mika. "We have bigger problems. We need to find a way to temporarily bind your magic. Wearing as many layers as you do looks suspicious. Gloves inside? Not subtle."

She wasn't wrong, but Mika still glared. "I'd rather not add to my body count."

"Then hurry up and get dressed so we can figure this shit out. I made eggs and crepes." Audrey slipped her hands in her pockets and gave Mika a wink. "And coffee is ready too, grumpy."

Mika threw a pillow but Audrey ducked out of the room with a laugh.

Grabbing her shower kit she made her way down the hall to the super fancy bathrooms she shared with her floor. A quick shower and she almost felt alive. Coffee should help her find the will to function.

Walking back to her room in nothing but a towel she glared at any guy who had the guts to look her up and down, smiling at her black bunny slippers.

Damn co-ed dorms.

She practically slammed the door closed behind her and went straight to her armoire. She should have brought her clothes with her, but if anyone touched her while she was wearing nothing but a towel, they would deserve what they got.

Slipping on her black, silk gloves first made her feel a little better. Mika hurried and jumped into a pair of her favorite black jeans and stuffed her feet into black sheepskin boots. The grey sweater she grabbed was one of her favorites and super warm.

Hesitating, Mika decided she'd rather be safe than sorry and grabbed a blanket scarf. She wrapped it around her neck and the lower half of her face. Almost every inch of skin was covered and the slight anxiety prickling under her skin eased.

Mika took the staircase down to the bottom floor,

eyeing the weather through the glass walls. Going to a party tonight really didn't sound like a good idea.

"In here!" Audrey called from their massive kitchen.

Sure they had to share it with about fifty other students, but it was so big and so many people had different schedules it didn't even matter. The black cupboards and stainless steel set off the cutting board counters.

Mika grabbed a stool and sat at the center island where Audrey had all the food set up.

"Let me guess, you take your coffee black just like your soul?" Audrey asked, pouring her a cup.

"Bold of you to assume I have a soul," Mika smirked, scooping eggs and crepes onto her plate.

Audrey set down the French press and stared at her. "Mika Marshall, did you just make a joke?"

"It's a strong possibility." Mika grabbed the bowl of sugar cubes – someone had bought black sugar cubes, how gauche – and tossed two into her cup. "I take two sugars and cream in my coffee."

Her dorm mate laughed and pushed the cream toward her before sitting down at her own plate. "I covered the books from the library with enchanted covers," Audrey murmured. "Unless someone feels like borrowing a book on penis magic or Suzie's Guide to Baking Love and Hate then they should leave them alone."

Mika almost spit out her coffee. "Penis magic?"

Audrey smiled over her, ironically, black coffee. "I

don't know if it's a thing, but hopefully it sounds just as repulsive to everyone else."

A few girls came into the kitchen chatting about whatever classes they had together, peered into the refrigerator, and then asked if there was more coffee. One of the dudes living in Oleander House came up behind the witches and scared them, making one spill coffee everywhere.

A pretty redhead laughed and said a few words, cleaning up the mess.

Mika felt strange watching them. She was an outsider to this normal existence and she knew without ever having to try that she would never fit in with them. They didn't have a care in the world other than homework and Fates knew what other mundane shit.

"Hey, did you know I'm the only human-born witch in this house?" Audrey whispered, following Mika's line of sight.

She shook her head and scooped strawberries from the greenhouse onto her crepes and then whipped cream. "There aren't many, but I doubt you're the only one in our freshman class."

"I'm not, but that doesn't make things easier." Audrey looked away from the group that was now studying them as well and took a bite of her eggs.

The guy was giving Mika strange looks for the scarf she'd pulled down, but was still bunched up under her chin, draping over her neck and shoulders. He nudged the redhead and they laughed like Mika was somehow hilarious.

She would care more if she didn't know how easy it would be to make their lives a living hell.

Mika took another sip of coffee and then scooped up a bite of strawberries and crepe.

"I was wondering," one of the girls said, coming over to lean on the island next to them. "How did you end up in Oleander House, Audrey? Usually it's reserved for the older clans."

The girl was gorgeous, with dark brown hair and green eyes. Mika thought her dark preppy look was cute and she definitely wanted to know where the other witch had gotten that skirt, but her bitch radar was going off.

"I was placed here by the Dean," Audrey said stiffly, setting down her fork.

The girl then looked at Mika and gave her a shitty grin. "So, it's not because your girlfriend is a Marshall? I mean, that's cool if it is. But don't lie to us."

Mika raised an eyebrow at this girl that reminded her of every rich bitch cliché that ever existed. "I didn't know Audrey before arriving at Morgana."

"It speaks!" the girl yelled, the sound forcing the others in the group to turn and look at them.

Her grip tightened on her cup, but Mika didn't look away or back down.

"I honestly thought you were mute," the redhead said, looking Mika up and down. "It really wouldn't have been surprising considering what happened to your coven."

Her hands were tingling and Mika carefully released her cup. She didn't need it exploding.

"Look, maybe you should mind your own business," Audrey snapped, crossing her arms over her chest. "We have five years to get through. You don't need to make it feel any longer than it already is."

"You're a mistake," the girl said, turning on Audrey. "You're nothing more than an accident of birth and you don't belong here."

Mika felt that coldness fill her veins – it was familiar and soothing. She picked up her coffee cup again with both hands and took a sip. "I suggest you find some other project than torturing Audrey."

"Oh?" She placed her hand on her hip and cocked it, raising her eyebrow at Mika while the others behind her watched on. "And what are you going to do if I don't?"

All Mika had to do was look at her.

The snotty bitch flew across the kitchen into her boy toy. A simple motion spell she'd compressed down until just thinking the words focused her power. Battle magic didn't require touching anyone.

"You bitch! How dare you!" The girl was struggling to get up, but Mika ignored her.

She took another sip of coffee and smiled. "If you don't stop, you're going to become *my* project."

The girl spluttered.

"Come on," the redhead said. "Let's go Crystal."

Of course her name was Crystal.

Mika watched them go, knowing this wouldn't be the last time.

But damn it felt good to remind them they weren't the only ones who could push people around.

Audrey took a bite of her eggs and studied Mika. They chewed in silence together and with the snow falling, the books to be read...Mika felt like maybe today was going to be a good day.

"You gotta teach me how you compress these spells down like that," Audrey finally said, sipping her coffee. "And remind me never to fuck with you."

"There's always one in every class," Mika told her. "And you belong here just as much as she does."

"You sure you don't want to be my girlfriend?"

Mika gave Audrey a half-smile. "I'm sure there's someone a lot less fucked up for you out there."

The other witch chuckled. "Aw, you know that would just be boring."

She supposed it probably would be. "Let's find something in those books that makes me look like less of a psycho."

Audrey got up and carefully picked up the edge of Mika's scarf to wrap it around the lower half of her face.

Mika glared. "I wasn't done eating."

"Let's go weirdo, I might have found something while you were snoozing."

"This spell seems..." Mika looked over the ingredients again and then the instructions – it was one of the few blood books in Latin.

"Gross?" Audrey asked, squinting to read the smudged incantation.

"Too easy." There wasn't a whole lot to it and Mika felt like it couldn't possibly work.

"Well, the only way to know for sure is to test it out." Audrey pulled a silver ingot out of her bag and set it on the table.

They were in one of the smaller common areas on the main floor – a study space with a stone table under glass walls like the conservatory. Mika loved it. They would have to redo their house in San Francisco to add some of these sun rooms.

"The silver has been blessed by a priestess – or so the package said in the campus store," Audrey told her.

Mika picked up the ingot and instantly recognized the smell of sage. "Says here in the spell it needs to be melted down from something precious. I don't think this is going to work."

And knowing how magic liked to exact a price, Mika reached into her bag.

"That's not silver," Audrey said. "It's black."

"It's made of silver," Mika promised. "And precious to me."

The other witch picked up the pen and read the transcription. "'To those who tried to burn us—shine bright – Dad.'" Audrey looked up with a frown. "I thought you hated him."

Mika took the pen back and set it into a stone bowl. "I do. And I keep this to remind me that evil hides in unlikely places. His words have made me strong – they've kept me going. But who I thought gave this to me – was not my actual father. I don't ever want to forget that."

They both stared at the pen in the bowl.

"Are you sure?" Audrey asked.

"Burn it down." Mika knew the price would be satisfactory. "I'm not fucking around with a blood spell."

Audrey waved her hand over the pen and muttered a few words. Instantly the pen grew white hot and then melted into a silvery puddle. "Well, if this works it seems fitting that we used your pen to do it."

"It seems similar to the spell the hunters use to temporarily bind a witch's power," Mika mused, flipping the page to see the illustration. "They spell cuffs and zip ties – that kind of thing."

"That's what I noticed too," Audrey said, pushing the bowl of melted down silver toward Mika. "But this is a lot simpler."

"Witch blood has a lot of power," Mika murmured. She took a pinch of snakeroot and added it to the silver to cleanse it. She muttered a quick prayer and then took the blade she'd been given at birth out of its case.

"Maybe we should go outside," Audrey whispered when Mika hesitated.

"It's fine," she hissed back. "Let's just get this over with."

Mika gritted her teeth and sliced her wrist carefully. There was no need to cut the tendons and one inch should do it. She murmured the incantation in Latin as she moved her hand over the bowl, letting her blood pour over the silver. "*With this, I bind you.*"

After a lifetime of being told dark magics were evil and taboo – that only witches with questionable morals used the darker magics – Mika felt that strange twinge of guilt and fear deep down as the blood and the silver started to bubble together.

She pressed her hand over the cut and watched with wide eyes as the blood was absorbed. The burst of smoke when the blood had first touched the liquid silver hadn't smelled unpleasant. Mika had been sure everything would smell like rot and death.

But it was just another spell – this one just happened to call for a witch's blood. And it didn't even ask for that much of it.

So, why did everyone freak out about blood magic?

Then the silver started to take shape, rising from the bowl. Both Audrey and Mika leaned back, unsure of what might happen next. The spell just said it would turn into something she could wear.

Clank.

Mika eyed the piece. "The book says it's supposed to take on a shape that represents the witch whose blood is used."

They stared at the silver.

"That's not foreboding or anything," Audrey muttered.

She handed the book over to Audrey and picked up the bracelet. "Definitely not promising," Mika agreed.

There was no trace of the blood that had been used and Mika's cut had already stopped bleeding. She wrapped it up once with healing gauze and secured it with some tape. Then she eyed the bracelet again.

It wasn't a normal bracelet. It clasped around the wrist, but that was where the similarities to typical bracelets ended. Coming from the circle bit were silver attachments similar to chains that connected to five rings. And the silver looked like bones. Once it was on, a skeleton would be over her hand.

"Not less conspicuous either," Mika muttered, finally picking it up.

"Want to test it out?" Audrey asked excitedly.

"Absolutely not." Mika glared at the other witch as she clasped it around her left wrist. She began removing her other rings and set them carefully on the table. "If I'm going to test it on anyone it's going to be Crystal, not you."

Audrey picked up one of her rings and inspected it. "I doubt you'll kill me."

"I said no." The rings of the bracelet fit on each finger perfectly from her pinky finger to her thumb. It was weird. And the metal was heavy. It left almost a physical weight on her chest Mika didn't particularly like.

"Okay, then show me how to compress magic the way you do." Audrey eyed the silver glittering under the snowy light. "I've never seen someone do it the way you do."

"It takes practice." Mika took off her other glove and inspected her hands. No tingles, and she didn't feel like she could hurt someone either. The weight on her chest was slowly easing as she got used to it, but she knew her connection to the universe was bound.

No magic unless she took it off.

"This is terrifying," she whispered, flexing her fingers. "I've never been completely cut off from magic before."

Audrey looked at the bracelet like it might burn her if she got too close. "So you won't be able to kill anyone with a touch, but you definitely can't try out for the Morgana Marauders either. We really need to sort out your block and shit. Is there a therapist on campus?"

The other witch started stacking the blood magic books and pulled out a battle magic book. Mika didn't know what to say as Audrey started flipping through the illustrations. She was right of course. Now Mika couldn't do any magic at all.

"I don't know if there's a therapist. But I wouldn't tell them about the blood magic even if I went to go see them." Mika grabbed a notebook from her bag and slid it over to Audrey. "Here are some of my basic equations. Each spell has its steps right? Well I take those steps and compress them. Then I practice until I can focus the magic correctly. Then I compress it again. And so on. It takes time, but it's doable. There are certain sigils and runes that I've already done the math for."

Audrey looked up from the notebook in shock. "You created your own sigils."

Mika shrugged. "Kind of. They're just combinations. It's not that hard to do, but not easy to perform if you don't have the concentration, or power."

"Holy shit, girl. Once you get that block removed, you're going to be unstoppable."

It was weird, looking at the notes she'd started over five years ago. Compressing spells had been one of her favorite projects and she'd been really good at it. Thank the Fates she'd never showed off her magic or projects. Claire had been brilliant and beautiful enough as the oldest to take up most of the attention.

Until she'd left. But even then Claire had been a stellar witch and their parents never stopped talking about her.

Staring at the notebook, Mika didn't feel like she'd ever be able to get through her mental block.

"Mika? Uh, they were looking for you," a small, quavering voice said.

Mika looked up and was somehow not surprised to see Kenzie standing there with her three hotties behind her. The frightened looking male witch scurried off when Kenzie grinned.

"Hello my witchy bitch."

16

Kenzie sat down at the stone table with that trademark 'I don't give a fuck' grin and Audrey and Mika just stared.

Then Audrey looked at the men still standing at the door, looking around the sun room like it smelled bad or something.

"So Eisheth told me we might end up cousins," Kenzie said. "Hence the nickname. We can work on it if you don't like it though."

Mika didn't know what to say. She just...had no words.

"Cousins?" she finally managed.

Kenzie shrugged and pulled the pile of books on the table closer to her. Audrey instantly grabbed them and yanked them back. The fox with the hair as bright red as Kenzie's growled and Audrey had the audacity to growl back.

"I already know about the blood thing. Eisheth is a gossipy bitch," Kenzie said. She crossed her arms over her chest and glared at Audrey. Then she turned that glare onto Mika. "Who's this?"

"Tell me how the hell we could possibly be cousins?" Mika demanded, crossing her own arms over her chest.

Kenzie Kavanagh didn't scare her.

If anything her powers as a void could be a blessing if Mika couldn't get her shit together.

The void witch rolled her eyes and looked over at her mates. "Eisheth is my demon godfather. He's also adopted a few others like us. The other day he popped in for his scheduled visit to train me and mentioned he heard whispers of his name at the University of Morgana."

Kenzie leaned forward to inspect the ingredients on the table, picking up the silver ingot.

A demon godfather.

Why did that sound so terrifying? Mika didn't need more people nosing into her life, let alone a damn demon.

"Anyways, Jess says it makes us cousins, so I figure that's what we're going to call it from now on." Kenzie grinned at Mika and then looked back at Audrey.

"I like her," the cocky redheaded dude said. "She's got good growl."

Mika wanted the earth to open up and swallow her whole. She had never had to interact with the void's mates, but that didn't mean she wanted to. They were nothing but chaos.

The quiet one came forward until they were barely an inch away from each other. This one had red hair so dark it was burgundy. Mika stared up at him – her entire body tense. She had no idea what he had planned, but it put her on edge.

Suddenly his hand snatched out too fast for her eyes to easily follow. He gripped her wrist and yanked it forward, peering at the silver bones. "This looks intriguing."

"Hunter, did you find a new friend?" the black-haired one asked, coming up behind Kenzie to put his hands on her shoulders.

The three of them made Mika feel caged. She yanked her hand out of Hunter's grip. "If you're so interested, maybe you'll volunteer to be my test subject."

Mika didn't expect Hunter to tilt his head at her, eyes flashing with amusement. The serious look on his face hid the truths she could see in those strange, gold eyes. "Test subject? If that's what you need." Hunter sat down next to her and held out his hand. "I've been a test subject before."

She shared a look with Audrey. This one was definitely psychotic.

"Why?" Mika asked.

Hunter didn't blink. It made her heart rate pick up – even without the bracelet binding her magic; this one would be hard to kill. "You're helping Kenzie. So I'm willing to help you."

Mika hadn't honestly expected Kenzie to take her up

on the offer. After all, the other witch was nearly a decade older than her. But...she'd meant what she'd said. Mika would do whatever she could to help Kenzie adjust.

Weirdos had to stick together.

"I could kill you," Mika warned him.

"Oh, this is definitely going to be my new favorite game," the cocky one said. He sat down at the large stone table with a grin and watched Mika eagerly.

Kenzie just smiled slightly. "You haven't met them officially, but these are my mates. Finnick." She pointed to the one who's hair matched hers—Fates, he was tall. "Ash." Kenzie placed her hand over the black-haired fox's hands, still resting on her shoulders. "And then Hunter."

Audrey shifted awkwardly.

"This is my dorm mate and friend, Audrey. She was born into a human family." Mika tilted her head slightly and eyed Hunter again. "Audrey, this is Kenzie who I'm sure you've already heard of. And I'm Mika."

Hunter's eyes flashed a glowing gold and then went back to his normal color. "A pleasure. Now, my mate hasn't explained your situation in detail." Then he tilted his head. "Why do you think you'll kill me?"

Mika looked at Audrey, and then at Kenzie. She wasn't sure what to say or do. She'd spent the last three years burying it all down deep.

"Bradley Davis assaulted her," Audrey said quietly. "She killed someone trying to make it back home from that experience. Now Mika has a block."

All three of the foxes growled at that and Kenzie's eyes widened in surprise. "You weren't on the list."

Mika glared at Audrey. "I never tried to report him for it."

"Why?"

Sighing, Mika wondered if she'd bitten off more than she could chew. But had she known *this* would be the result of agreeing to help Kenzie...

She'd probably still do it.

"Because I didn't want to hurt Selene," Mika said quietly. "I'd just turned sixteen and she was still engaged to him. I didn't know I wasn't the only one." Hunter's hand was still on the table, waiting for her to take it.

The void witch look pissed, but she also seemed to understand. "Selene is stronger than we give her credit for."

"She is," Mika agreed. "I still couldn't tell anyone."

"Because of who you killed?" Ash asked.

"No," Mika snapped, hating how vulnerable this conversation made her feel.

She glanced at Audrey and the other witch whispered a few words, twisting her fingers just once. A silencing spell sealed the room.

"Thank you."

"No problem."

"Fuck!" Finnick shouted, making her and Audrey jump. "I really do not like the smell of magic."

"Maybe you shouldn't be talking about how I killed people like *no one can hear you* then," Mika snapped, crossing her arms over her chest again and glaring. "It's not because of *who* I killed," Mika finally said, glancing at Kenzie. "But how."

"Show me," Hunter demanded.

Mika looked at Kenzie again for permission. The void witch chewed on her bottom lip in concern, but nodded.

"I could really hurt him," Mika warned.

Mates were no joke and Mika *really* didn't want the backlash from this.

"If you lose control I'll drain you," Kenzie promised, flexing her fingers. "Don't worry, I can give it back."

Mika nodded and then flexed her own hand, eyeing the silver. She unclasped the bracelet and slid each ring off. The weight instantly lifted and her power rose up in relief. It took a minute to clear her head and regain control of it all.

Something to remember if she ever took the bracelet off again.

Then Mika stared into Hunter's golden brown eyes, wondering what kind of person was curious enough to submit himself to this.

Gently she placed her hand in his still waiting one – this fox had infinite patience. Mika didn't dare look away from him, even as her fingertips started to tingle. She wasn't currently frightened or worked up so the magic didn't rise up on its own.

Mika imagined the blood in his veins, pumping through his body, and then she whispered to it.

The sharp tang of blood filled the air and the red liquid started dripping from between their hands. It pooled on the stone table, growing wider and wider. It felt like a release to finally use her powers on purpose.

Hunter grew pale and sweat started to bead on his

forehead, but still he didn't blink or look down at their hands. His gaze kept her grounded and Mika gritted her teeth, forcefully yanking her hand back despite the sweet draw of the magic.

She looked down and studied the blood covering her hand, trying not to panic. "Did it hurt?"

"No, actually," Hunter admitted. "Though I imagine it could if you were afraid or panicking—or wanted it to."

Everyone leaned forward to study the blood on Hunter's hand, there was enough of it to pool onto the table.

A snap of Audrey's fingers and the blood on the table turned to ash. "You don't want it just...around," she explained.

"I like her," Ash murmured, massaging Kenzie's shoulders. "Would it be rude to ask Eiseth exactly how many cousins he's planning on giving you?"

Kenzie laughed and pressed her knuckles to Hunter's forehead to feel how clammy he was, leaning across Mika. "I don't think he even knows."

She really wished they would stop saying his name.

"I don't think I've ever heard of a blood witch," Hunter said. "But I could contact some of the foxes I know and see what they have in our archives."

"I would appreciate that." Mika took a napkin and carefully wiped the blood from her hand. "So, what can I help you with Kenzie?"

"Would you babysit my foxes while I take my class?"

Instantly Mika went still. She shot a look at Audrey. "Babysit them?"

Kenzie shrugged. "Yeah, they can't take my class with me since they're shifters and aren't allowed to enroll, but they refuse to let me come here alone. They need entertaining."

Finnick rolled his eyes and sighed loudly. "We're not children."

The void witch kicked his chair. "I'm giving you a blood witch to play with, be thankful."

"Who can do battle magic," Audrey said. "She's training me actually. Tryouts are tomorrow."

It was Mika's turn to kick Audrey's chair under the table. Her dorm mate kept throwing her under the damn bus.

"Battle magic?" Ash asked, perking up. "There's a team? This sounds like fun."

Hunter smiled lazily as he took the napkin from Mika and wiped the remaining blood from his hand as well. "Eisheth asked that we help you as well, Mika."

"Please stop saying his name," Mika gritted out. How the hell was she supposed to babysit these three, tutor Audrey, and get all her homework done every week? "Look, I have homework and shit. How am I possibly going to entertain them?"

Kenzie grinned. "I'm sure you'll think of something, cuz." She stood up and blew Mika a kiss. "I have a four hour class. That's it. Only four hours. I believe in you."

The void witch left the sun room, dissolving the silence spell as it touched her – absorbing it into her body from the feel of the magic.

Audrey and Mika stared at the foxes, unsure what to do next.

"Hungry?" Audrey asked, snapping her fingers with a single word to burn up the bloody napkin.

Ash grinned and somehow it mirrored the feral one on Finnick's face. "Always."

17

B abysitting three grown-ass foxes wasn't as easy as it should have been. Hunter wouldn't give her back her bracelet, and Audrey spent an hour cooking for them while Mika quizzed her on Latin.

Surprisingly, Hunter knew Latin as well as Mika did so she'd handed him the textbook and moved on to her own homework. The alpha fox had looked surprised – in his own way – when she'd given him the responsibility.

"So explain what a block is," Ash said, shoveling his second helping of Audrey's cooking into his mouth – more crepes.

Mika ignored him. This wasn't supposed to be about her. "When you are all done eating we should take a walk around the island."

"Do you have any boyfriends?" Finnick asked Audrey, staring up at her like she was some kind of kitchen goddess.

"I can't even get one girlfriend," Audrey smirked. "*Multiple* girlfriends seems impossible."

"Find yourself some lesbian cat shifters," Ash said. "Problem solved."

"Except they have to be mates," Mika muttered, writing down the answer to her last interdimensional physics equation.

"Anyone ever tell you you're a buzzkill, Mika?" Finnick asked, pushing his empty plate back.

Witches kept walking by the kitchen, whispering and staring at them. Kenzie had gotten everyone's attention and now she'd left her three shifter mates with the crazy bitch and the human-born witch.

Mika glared at the group of freshmen and they scuttled off. "You're certainly not the first, Finnick."

Ash raised his eyebrows. "Sassy."

"We have a lot of work to do," Mika said, pulling at her gloves. Not having her bracelet was making her uncomfortable. She glared at Hunter again, but he just ignored her and checked Audrey's conjugation.

"Don't worry, babe, this is my last bit of homework," Audrey told her. "Then we can train."

"I want to see battle magic," Finnick pouted. "Hurry up."

Mika almost missed the days when she was lonely and isolated.

She picked up one of her blood magic books and started reading from where she'd last left off.

"Penis magic?" Ash exclaimed.

"I don't think the people in the other dorm heard

you," Mika stated, turning the page. "Say it louder next time."

Finnick snorted and Hunter peered over her shoulder. "This one of the books on your specialty?" the alpha fox asked.

"Yes."

There was thirty seconds of blessed silence and then Finnick said, "Kenzie has blood charms."

Mika slammed the book closed and checked the doors to the kitchen. "Could you please *shut up*? I don't want people knowing," she hissed. "This kind of magic is considered dark."

"I thought Kenzie had a temper," Finnick muttered.

"All right, I'm done. Let's get the fuck out of here before Mika blows up the dormitory." Audrey slammed her books closed and slipped them in her bag. "I'll run these upstairs and then we can go." Her dorm mate held out her hand for Mika's book.

She couldn't get away from all the listening ears and curious glances. It put her on edge and she hated it. The only reason she hadn't already lost control was everyone was way more interested in the foxes than they were her.

"Hurry up," Mika said, handing Audrey the blood magic book. "I'm not a certified babysitter."

Hunter handed the Latin textbook over and eyed Mika like she was a tiny specimen that was surprisingly interesting.

She glared back at him. "Can I have my bracelet back?"

"You don't even know if it works," Hunter told her.

Mika held out her hand. "Are you offering to be my test subject again?"

"If you need me to be." Hunter didn't give her back the bracelet though. "You won't be able to do battle magic if you wear it."

"Audrey is the one trying out." Mika tried to snatch it out of his grip, but Hunter was too fast and held it just out of her reach.

"Let's go!" Audrey appeared in the kitchen entrance looking disheveled from running up and down all those stairs so quickly. She tossed Mika's coat to her and jerked her head at the main entrance to their dorm. "The sooner we get out of here the better."

Mika agreed. Three foxes cooped up in her dorm somehow made the massive house feel tiny.

Pulling on her coat she walked past Audrey and made a beeline for the door. Mika couldn't wait to breathe in that freezing cold air and get some space between her and everyone else. Purposefully pulling the blood from Hunter's skin had woken up her magic and it was pushing at her to *do* something.

She needed that damn bracelet back. Glaring at Hunter over her shoulder she pushed the door open and stepped outside.

Instantly the noise seemed to die down and Mika looked up at the cloudy, overcast sky. The sun was bright enough it wasn't dark outside despite the storm brewing. Was Ethan somehow responsible? She should check on him soon.

Mika could practically feel her skin soaking up the

rays. Closing her eyes she breathed deep, smelling the pine and the ocean.

The power in her veins settled a bit and she flexed her gloved fingers, easing the rest of the sensation.

"It really is beautiful here," Hunter said quietly.

Finnick, Ash, and Audrey were arguing about what penis magic could potentially do if it were real as they all pushed past her.

Mika opened her eyes and narrowed them at Hunter, pulling her scarf up and over her mouth and nose. "I heard you were a scary asshole."

Then he smiled and she could see the sharpness of his teeth up close. "I am."

She eyed him and those teeth. His creepy smile was sharp and promised pain and death. But then Mika looked into his eyes. They were soft and gentle and kind when he looked at her. They filled with love and adoration when he looked at Kenzie.

What did this one want from her?

"You're not scary," Mika told him. "Or an asshole."

That grin widened and she could easily picture blood dripping from those canines.

"I like you." Hunter turned to look at the trees that were the beginning of the little forest on the island. "You're not afraid of anything. Except yourself." The flash of gold in his eyes came and went so fast she thought maybe she'd imagined it. "You're helping Kenzie. So, I'm going to help you." The way he repeated that, it was like he was trying to convince himself, not her.

"Are you guys coming?" Audrey called back. She

practically ran through the snow with Ash and Finnick toward the trees and the cemetery hidden among them.

Mika fell into step next to Hunter. "How are you, a fox – no offense – going to help me?"

Hunter slipped his hands into his pockets as they walked. He was about the same height as her, maybe a little taller, which was kind of weird. Mika wasn't used to being at eye-level with men.

The way he looked at everything told her he was constantly alert even though there was no chance anything could come after them here – not with all the wards centuries of witches had placed on the school.

"Blocks come in many shapes and forms," Hunter finally said. "A therapist could fumble around and try to help you. Or you could get help from someone who can taste and read pain."

Mika stumbled and nearly fell. "What?"

"Foxes feed on chaos and pain," Hunter said simply, reaching out to steady her.

She jerked out of his grip, still not comfortable with anyone touching her. "How does that help me?"

He tilted his head at her then and smiled slightly. "Blocks are caused by pain. I can take that pain from you."

That winter quiet settled around her again as she stared at Hunter in disbelief. "It's not that simple," she whispered.

"No," he agreed. "But it would be a good start."

Mika narrowed her eyes in suspicion. "Did that demon put you up to this?"

Hunter growled slightly and started walking again. "As if that demon could make me do anything."

At least they had that in common, and for some reason that made her feel better.

This shifter was going to help her.

Mika shook her head. Help had come from the most unexpected place – and all thanks to the threads that connected them. Kenzie had watched Mika and Selene grow up together, always there but always an outsider.

Then a demon had heard her say his name in the deepest bowels of the university and for some reason had been interested enough to check in on her. Instead of tearing Mika into tiny pieces when he'd showed up, he'd even given her a few book recommendations.

And thanks to that and Kenzie...a fox shifter, a supposed *lesser shifter*, was here willing to help her get rid of her block when she couldn't trust anyone else – even with the contention between witches and shifters.

"Thank you," Mika whispered, knowing Hunter could hear her with that shifter hearing of his.

His eyes flashed gold and then went back to normal again, even though he didn't even glance at her. Mika appreciated the silence more than she would have a spoken acknowledgement.

"Are you ready?" Audrey called through the trees. And the words seemed to echo from everywhere at once.

Mika smiled slightly as the trees whispered their response.

For the first time in three years she felt like maybe—

just maybe, she could find a way to control her magic, and regain everything she'd lost.

18

The cemetery was just as peaceful as it always was. Mika trailed her fingers over the top of one of the headstones, wishing for just a second that she could feel the snow. Brushing it off the top she went around to see whether it was a John or a Jane Doe.

Hunter never strayed too far from her. Mika wondered what his deal was. Clearly he had something in mind to help her through her block. Not only that, he wasn't ready to give her back her bracelet. She wondered what that was about.

"Okay so, the opposite team stands behind the midfield line," Audrey was explaining to Ash and Finnick. "There are fifteen of us on each team." She started drawing lines in the snow and the other two foxes watched, completely fascinated.

"Not interested in battle magic dodgeball?" Mika asked Hunter, crouching in front of the grave to read the inscription. Some of them were super creepy.

None of the foxes were wearing coats. Hunter watched Audrey draw more lines in the snow, hands in his pockets. He shrugged one shoulder. "The concept is interesting. A healthy outlet for violence is something I don't think anyone should take for granted."

Mika looked up at him in surprise. She supposed he was right.

In loving memory of John CCDV, his bones were the sweetest addition to my spell.

She stood and frowned down at the headstone. Who was in charge of these epitaphs?

"Not everyone needs a healthy outlet for violence," Mika murmured, turning back to watch Audrey draw the other lines.

Hunter just gave her a look that said '*don't lie to yourself.*'

Mika rolled her eyes. These fucking foxes were so invasive.

"So then, it's basically dodgeball," Audrey explained. "But so much crazier than in the human world. The team of fifteen is completely free to form up however they want as long as they follow the rules and guidelines. Non-lethal spells only, and they keep that to fifteen different offensive spells including, get this, *fire*. Three shields total."

Ash eyed the length and width of the cemetery as she talked, as if imagining the whole thing.

"*Unlike* in human dodgeball," Audrey said, now bouncing up and down on the balls of her feet in excitement. "You're not considered 'out' until you're knocked off the court and into the water."

"You should try out for the team," Hunter said quietly.

"Are you saying that as my wannabe mentor, or as some dude I'm supposed to be babysitting?" Mika glared at nothing in particular, wishing she had shifter speed so she could take her damn bracelet back.

"You could take it from me right now if you weren't too afraid to use your own power," Hunter murmured, looking up as an owl flew overhead.

How he knew what she was thinking...Mika didn't bother asking. He was a weird guy.

"I want to see what you can do," Hunter told her, jerking his head at Audrey. "Play a round with her and I'll give you back your bracelet."

Mika looked at the other witch and Audrey was grinning as Finnick showed her a move to combine with a spell. Her eyes were bright and her cheeks rosy from the cold. This girl had spent most of her teenage years in a psych ward being told magic wasn't real and that she was just insane.

If she could get through that and come out the other side...maybe Mika could as well.

"One round," Mika agreed. "But you have to let me test if the bracelet works on you."

Hunter's grin was sharp as he placed the silver bone bracelet on top of the nearest headstone. "Agreed."

Tightening the scarf around her face and tying off one of the ends, Mika walked over to her side of the court and gave Audrey a nod. "Force me to shield," Mika told her. "Use my weakness against me."

Finnick and Ash grinned, jogging over to join Hunter to watch from the edge of the makeshift court.

Mika kept her gloves on, but slipped off her coat so she could move more easily. Despite being a game that uses magic, it was extremely physical. If she couldn't dodge or attack, Audrey would win. Mika's shields were little more than tissue paper.

As Audrey drew a spell into the air for the timer, Mika closed her eyes and took a deep breath, evaluating the state of her magic. After everything it was surprisingly acquiescent. It didn't push at her or make her feel like she might just kill everyone if she got mad.

Thank Fates for all the yoga she'd done. Meditating was the only thing that had helped her manage over the years.

Three years.

And it wasn't until she'd found out her father and brother had plans to take over the coven with Bradley Davis that she'd started to lose control again – unable to focus.

Had they known he was a rapist?

The bell went off and Mika's eyes flew open. Audrey's fingers were already painting runes into the air and Mika moved. A single movement and she sent a ball of energy at her dorm mate who blocked it with one hand, still building the offensive spell with the other.

She *had* been practicing.

Mika smiled under her scarf and sent two more

bursts of energy at Audrey, but the other witch had top notch defensive skills. Mika could wear her down or maneuver Audrey into a situation where her concentration was broken, weakening her spells.

Fire was always scary when it was coming right at your face. Mika hadn't had the opportunity to compress this spell as much. She made the two signs and spoke a single word, just barely managing to dodge the attack spell from Audrey. It hit one of the headstones behind her and the sound of the stone cracking was loud in the clearing.

Finnick and Ash were cheering them both on and Mika felt adrenaline coursing through her veins.

She'd missed this – the constant moves and counter moves required to play this game.

Taking a step forward advanced her toward Audrey, making the other witch feel defensive if Audrey's complex attack spell was any indication. Mika's eyes widened at the combination of three spells and dove just in time to avoid the crackling blast.

A swipe of her hand in the snow and one word caught Audrey at the ankles and the witch landed on her back. But her shield was still too strong and deflected Mika's next attack.

"You need to get me on the defensive!" Mika yelled. "Stop shielding all the time. Build your power quicker and send the spells faster. You need to be *faster!*"

Audrey blasted another spell at Mika as she flipped back onto her feet – moving as she sent blasts around her shield.

The amount of improvement she'd had in just a week was astounding. Audrey was already able to use each hand for a different spell and do it while on the move.

"Yes!" Mika sent attack after attack toward Audrey. One blasted at the shield and the other met Audrey's attack midway.

Mika couldn't shield, but she could fight fire with fire.

Audrey grinned when she realized what Mika was doing. She dropped her shield and sent another blast of pure energy into the air.

Snow fell from the tree and dropped right down on Mika. Her eyes widened as she saw two spells coming for her at once. She crossed her forearms and spoke a single word in Sumerian – knowing it wasn't going to hold.

The shield shimmered red just before the balls of energy blasted into her.

Mika flew back several feet and slammed into a headstone. It knocked the breath out of her and she sat there coughing, trying to get air back into her lungs.

"Mika!" More than one person yelled her name and she brushed the snow off her legs, still trying to breathe.

Hunter offered her his hand and she took it, letting him drag her to her feet.

"Are you okay?" Audrey asked, grabbing Mika by the shoulders and looking her up and down for damage. "Holy shit, I can't believe I actually got you."

She smiled at the other witch. "I'm out of practice and you're really good. I think you're ready."

"Mika!"

Looking over Audrey's shoulder she saw Ethan

jogging toward them from the tree line. Hunter growled behind her.

"Be nice," she hissed.

"That was insane," Ethan told her, glancing at the foxes before focusing on her. "I didn't realize you could play."

"A little," Mika said, making sure her gloves were still in place. She took a step back as Ethan got too close. "How are you feeling?"

"Much better despite nearly dying," he said with a smirk, noting the scarf and the gloves. Ethan took the hint and didn't try to get any closer. He watched as Ash and Finnick approached and then glanced at Hunter behind her. "Friends of yours?"

"I'm babysitting them," Mika told him.

The look on his face was worth it.

Ethan's jaw dropped. "Excuse me, what?"

"They're Kenzie's," Mika explained, lips twitching as she tried not to laugh.

Audrey didn't even bother; she was laughing so hard tears streamed down her face.

Mika rolled her eyes, but she smiled as Audrey leaned on Finnick when he got closer so she could wipe the tears from her face before they froze. "Kenzie is taking Friday classes. We're...friends. These are her mates – Hunter, Finnick, and Ash. Apparently they need babysitting."

Hunter grinned and stepped forward, smiling that terrifying smile at Ethan. To his credit, Ethan didn't back down, but he didn't look exactly comfortable either. "Shifters? Cool, what kind of shifters are you?"

"Foxes," Ash answered. "What kind of witch are you?"

No doubt the fox meant it as a jab, but Ethan smirked. "I'm a storm witch."

"Play nice," Mika warned.

"How do you know Mika?" Hunter asked, taking a step forward, maneuvering slightly in front of her.

She rolled her eyes.

They knew each other for all of a day and they were already interrogating boys for her.

Ethan actually laughed. "We have Advanced Poisons together and she almost killed me when she kissed me." He gave Mika a wink. "Worth it."

Finnick snorted. "He's as dumb as we are."

Hunter still didn't move out of the way. "What are your intentions?"

Mika punched Hunter right in the back, but his only reaction was to glare at her over his shoulder. "It's nothing serious," Mika told him. "Leave him alone. I'm the one who's supposed to be babysitting *you*."

"Ouch," Ethan said with a chuckle. "It's cool Mika; I can play the long game."

"Definitely stupid," Ash agreed.

"But hot as hell," Finnick said, looking Ethan up and down. "He's taller than I am. I like it."

For the first time since they met, she saw Ethan blush. He cleared his throat and avoided Finnick's scrutiny as much as he could.

Mika was glad the scarf covered her face, hiding her grin. "I like them tall," she agreed. Fates, Ethan was adorable. And still alive by some miracle.

"I was going to come see you at Oleander House," Ethan said, eyeing Finnick as he took another step toward Mika. "But then I heard the shouts and came to see what was going on. Are you going to try out tomorrow?"

"Just me," Audrey said, leaning against one of the headstones with a smirk. "Mika has been kind enough to train me though."

"Why aren't you going to try out?" Ethan asked, easing around Hunter.

It was ballsy of him and the way he pretended like the fox didn't even exist was kind of hot. Hunter could be scary when he wanted to be.

"Yeah Mika," Finnick said with a smirk. "Why aren't you trying out?"

"My little problem," Mika told Ethan, wriggling her gloved fingers at him. "I can't afford to accidentally touch anyone, and thanks to my block I can't shield for shit."

Hunter's watch went off and he finally broke eye contact with the back of Ethan's head. "Kenzie is on her way back from class. We should head back to the dorm."

Ethan reached out and took her gloved hand, eyes locked with hers and Mika couldn't look away despite all the eyes on them. She'd been really worried about Ethan, and then she'd felt weird about seeing him after he'd been discharged from the infirmary.

How did you reach out after nearly killing someone?

'Hey, sorry about that. Would you like to maybe grab a coffee? Funny how you're still breathing.'

Hunter stared at their hands and then he frowned. "How are you feeling right now?" he asked her.

Mika instantly released Ethan, feeling even weirder. "What are you talking about?"

"When you held his hand," Hunter said. "Did you feel like you were going to lose control?"

Audrey, Finnick, and Ash looked at her with interest – like this was all some sort of fascinating reality TV show.

"No, Hunter," Mika snapped. "I didn't feel like I was going to murder him. Can I have my damn bracelet back?"

The fox tossed it to her with a nod. Mika was surprised he'd held up his end of the deal. "I'm going to see what I can find in the archives," Hunter said, turning to head back to Oleander House. "We'll be back tomorrow."

She sighed and glanced at Ethan, who was grinning like an idiot. Finnick pounded him on the back and whispered something into Ethan's ear. Then he followed after his alpha fox with Ash trailing behind him.

"I just wanted to check on you," Ethan said, glancing at Audrey who was smiling at him with no intention of leaving so they could have some privacy. "Do you have time for coffee or something?"

Mika glanced at Audrey. She wasn't a flake. "I have plans," she said, inclining her head toward her dorm mate. "Maybe we can do coffee tomorrow or Sunday."

"I would like that." Ethan gave Audrey a nod and then leaned forward to kiss Mika's cheek over the scarf. "I'll text you to set up a time."

She watched him walk away, feeling her stomach flutter. Those shoulders... "It's still not serious!" she called after him.

Ethan waved without looking back and Audrey burst out laughing. Her dorm mate linked her arm through hers and pulled her after the foxes. "Let's go test this bracelet on Hunter."

19

Kenzie was taking interdimensional physics too. Something about a missing portal or whatever. But she'd decided to leave at the break halfway through the class since she already knew most of the work.

She'd picked up her foxes and headed to the library, promising to visit again next week.

Without all their chaos it felt oddly quiet in their dormitory.

Audrey and Mika sat on one of the couches in front of a massive fireplace and sipped at Audrey's brandy hot chocolate.

"Hoes over bros," Audrey finally said.

Mika nearly spat out her hot chocolate. "I promised you I would go to that stupid party tonight and I wanted time to get ready. Bros and hoes have nothing to do with it."

Audrey sipped her hot chocolate, eyes twinkling over the cup. "Ethan is super cute. I see why you like him."

He was definitely hot.

Going out with Ethan was probably a mistake, but she'd nearly killed him and he still wanted to hang out with her. That had to count for something. Even her 'no boyfriends' rule had to take a back seat for that.

"It's nothing serious," Mika said again.

"What do you think it would be like to have three significant others?" Audrey asked. "Do you think they have to like, schedule things, or...not?"

Mika watched the log pop in the fire and a spark rose up the chimney like a lazy snowflake – opposite in every way. "I've no idea, but it works for the feline shifters."

"Do you really think it would work with people who weren't mated?" Audrey asked.

She eyed her dorm mate. "Are you asking because you want to date more than one girl?"

Audrey laughed and pushed Mika with her socked foot. "I'm just curious! And you're the one with multiple boys drooling all over you. Ethan and then Lucien. I bet you Malachi would be interested too. If he didn't think you were gay."

The whole universe was conspiring against her.

Mika smiled slightly and set down her mug. "And I could accidentally kill them all."

"Hey! Not anymore." Audrey grabbed Mika's bare hand and shook it. "We know the bracelet works, thanks to Hunter."

It was a blood spell. Of course it worked. The power infused into the silver was considerable. But still...Mika had doubted.

"Do you really think they'll come tomorrow?" Mika asked.

Audrey sighed and set down her mug as well. "I hope so. For some reason I get the feeling that if anyone is going to get you through this block, it's going to be that psycho."

"Yeah, probably. Like calls to like and all that," Mika muttered.

"Truer words," Audrey laughed. "So, what can I do to get you to try out for the team?"

Mika considered what Hunter had said. Maybe having an outlet for all her anger and rage wasn't a bad idea. But with her issues shielding and generally being out of practice...she wouldn't make the team.

"You would have to go back in time to when I first got here, convince me to try out, remove my block so I could shield, and then make me practice eight hours a day," Mika said with a shrug, stretching out across the couch, throwing her legs across Audrey's lap. The warmth from the fire felt perfect and for the first time all week she didn't have to wear a hundred layers inside. "I'm not good enough to make a university level team right now. It's been three years since I played."

The other witch grumbled under her breath but didn't argue. "You don't have to be perfect. That's the whole reason we have so much practice before our first game." Audrey tapped Mika's knees. "You are good enough for a spring season. And you don't necessarily need to shield if you use offensive spells to block."

The fire crackled again and Mika thought about it.

Spring session broke up a team of eighty players into four teams. They played against each other all spring until the last game. The best players were then handpicked to join the Marauders for the fall season when they would play against the other branches of the University of Morgana.

"I'll think about it," she promised Audrey. "Depending on how tonight goes."

"I know it's cold as fuck outside, but it'll be warm inside the hunters' dormitory," Audrey said, a grin spreading across her face. "Now that you don't have to layer up, how sexy do you want to get tonight?" She tapped Mika's legs. "How badly do you want to make those boys lose their minds?"

Three years of keeping her distance and wearing clothes that covered most of her skin...Mika smiled slightly. It would be nice to wear some of the stuff she used to. "I've actually got something in mind," she told Audrey. "Want to get ready?"

Audrey glanced at her phone. "We have three hours before the party starts."

Mika shrugged. "Getting ready is the best part. Come on, bring some wine or something. I'll do your makeup."

The way the other witch lit up was worth it. Mika hadn't had a friend in a long time. She'd missed this.

"Yes!" Audrey exclaimed. "You always look amazing. That smoky eye suits you, but I don't know if it'll work on me." Audrey shoved Mika's legs off her lap and hopped up. "I'll get the wine and meet you upstairs."

Mika got up slowly and stretched.

She almost hadn't come to the university. She'd applied in her senior year of high school of course because that's what was expected of her. But when she'd gotten her acceptance letter Mika had sat on it for a long time.

How could she possibly go to a university to learn higher magic if she couldn't do a simple illumination spell?

So she'd deferred and then all hell had broken loose with her coven.

Mika had almost sent the dean an apology stating she couldn't attend at all, but Takahashi had convinced her to try at least one year.

One year.

And it was the best decision she'd made in a long time.

Not only did Mika have a friend, she was breaking out of her shell. She was finding answers and solutions. It no longer felt like she was drowning in her secrets, in the fear of what she could do.

She had a lot of work to do still, but Mika felt like she was making progress. And that, that was a huge thing after three years of hiding.

It was a miracle she'd even gotten through high school. Mika didn't want to think about how she'd managed it.

No, this was a new beginning and it was time to start moving on from all that shit.

Mika picked up their empty mugs and headed toward

the kitchen, humming as she considered how to do Audrey's makeup.

Finally, it felt like she could breathe again.

***

"Okay, I think that should do it," Mika said, dusting the excess powder off of Audrey's face.

Her dorm mate had insisted on watching Mika do her own first. But makeup was one of those things she'd gotten really good at over the years. It was now her favorite hobby after quitting the dodgeball team at her school.

Audrey turned and looked in the mirror. "Holy shit, I look like a fierce femme. Gah, you used magic didn't you?"

Mika smiled at that. "You know I didn't. You're gorgeous Audrey, and you don't need makeup to look femme."

"I tend to dress like a tomboy even though I'm not butch," Audrey admitted, moving her head from side to side to admire the wings of her eyeliner and the way the highlighter glowed under the light. "I wish I was better at this stuff."

"I can teach you if you want," Mika said with a shrug, putting her makeup away. Audrey had opted out of the bold eyeshadow look Mika had on – deep red with thick black eyeliner. "But you're beautiful and any girl would be lucky to have you, makeup or not."

Audrey turned and Mika could feel the other witch studying her from head to toe.

The chunky boots Mika wore had a silver pentagram

clasp, and her thigh high stockings would add a little warmth to her outfit. Her black skirt was short and flirty – totally preppy. The burgundy sweater only added to the schoolgirl look, but it showed just enough cleavage to remind everyone she wasn't in high school anymore.

The bone bracelet didn't really match her ensemble, but Mika wasn't taking it off, so she had a silver necklace with real bones dangling from it – runes carved into them for protection and power.

"You're going to make someone's nose bleed," Audrey finally said, adjusting her hair cuff. It was a savagely feminine gold piece that wrapped around Audrey's bun and reminded Mika of some kind of pagan goddess.

Mika finished the last of her wine and it warmed her blood. Thanks to the bone bracelet though her magic didn't rise up – she felt it sleeping under the weight of the silver and it eased her anxiety to normal levels.

Normal – whatever that meant.

"If someone's nose bleeds, I'll try out for the team." Mika smirked at Audrey and set the wineglass down on the vanity. "You ready to go?"

"Challenge accepted," Audrey said with a laugh. "But you still have to consider trying out! For real, and not just as a joke."

Audrey grabbed her coat and Mika adjusted the other witch's dress. "I told you I will. This dress is perfect." She smoothed Audrey's collar and stepped back. "You look sexy."

Her dorm mate grinned and tossed Mika her coat. "Back at you, witchy bitch."

She couldn't help but smile at that.

They headed down the stairs together, eyeing the others who were getting ready for the party as well. Audrey and Claire hadn't been lying when they said this party was legendary.

"Is everyone on campus going?" Mika asked, noticing how empty the common areas were. They pushed open the massive doors to the wintery night and small groups were laughing and joking as they all headed to the same place.

"Everyone," Audrey told her. "It's one of those things – the hunters aren't all witches so they don't discriminate. Doesn't matter if you're from Oleander House or Sage House, everyone is welcome."

Mika liked the sound of that. "I wish that attitude spread to the witches," she muttered. "Something needs to change."

Audrey glanced at her. "What do you mean?"

They stayed on the paths where the snow had been plowed and followed the other groups of students toward the music they could hear clear across the island.

"Witches have insanely stupid prejudices toward shifters," Mika told her. "Shifters don't trust us because of it. We're supposed to be neutral, yet working with other paranormals is almost impossible. They buy magic from us and still hate us. We help some, and not others...they're not even allowed to attend this university. The hunters were let in only two hundred years ago," she explained. "Be grateful you grew up without all this crap."

"Witches don't like us human-borns," Audrey reminded her. "I've been made painfully aware of this over the last year."

"That too," Mika agreed, linking her arm with Audrey's. "Though I think that's just jealousy. A lot of human-born witches are very powerful. And there have been more of them over the last few decades."

Audrey led them through the trees toward the hunter's dorm, the stone path slick enough they walked slowly. "It's weird that there are born hunters, and then there are people who just decide to be hunters – witches, humans..."

Mika thought of Lucien and wondered what he would be classified as. Not that she really cared, she was just...intrigued.

Who was he and why was he so damn fast?

"We should petition to let others attend," Audrey said after they passed another group. "Shifters can't do magic, but we all live in the same world. There are half-demons...who knows what else. If they qualify as a paranormal – they should be allowed to study here. They let in Kenzie, the first void witch in forever."

A void witch.

Nothing like her at all – and yet, more alike than one would assume.

"It took the Council of Paranormals overruling the university's decision to get Kenzie in," Mika admitted, glancing up when an owl hooted at them. At least it wasn't snowing. "That kind of change would require changing the rules, or replacing those on the board opposing the idea."

The music grew louder and even though it was pitch black outside, Mika could see perfectly. Each branch of each tree was in perfect focus. The snow was crystalized and the light from the dorm made it glitter as they grew closer.

The two of them paused outside the hunter's dormitory, letting others push past them.

"Imagine what we could accomplish if we worked together." Audrey smirked. "Let's go make some noses bleed."

20

The hunter's dormitory was even bigger than Oleander House, but it made sense. It was the original building for the school and housed all the hunters attending the university. No doubt it was to help them study and practice with other students working on the same specialty, but it still felt weird to Mika that they were all kept to one dorm.

Most didn't take any classes the witches did. There were a few basic intro classes that allowed for some crossover, but Morgana was definitely geared toward witches and everything else was an afterthought.

She climbed up those stairs with Audrey, noticing that some witch must have spelled the stone so ice didn't stick to the stairs. Either there was a witch training to become a hunter, or someone had witch friends.

The dorm radiated a warmth that combatted the freezing night air and Mika slipped off her coat, handing it over to whatever freshman was in charge of the coats that night.

If the University of Morgana had something like a 'frat' house, this would be it.

But she was pleased to see there was a good amount of female hunters as well based on the class pictures hanging in the massive entryway.

There was something different about this dormitory. Mika felt it in the air.

It was a home and the hunters had this camaraderie the witches didn't have, even when they lived in the same house.

Audrey was already laughing with someone as she handed over her coat. The music was so loud Mika didn't know how anyone could hold a conversation. Alcohol was served at various different bars along with the kegs that were set up in strategic places.

Someone had even posted an itinerary on the wall next to the coat check. Apparently a band was going to play outside at some point. There were games in various locations, and food in the kitchen.

It was fancy and Mika could see why this party was legendary.

"I didn't think you would show," a sly voice whispered in her ear.

Mika looked up to see Lucien behind her and her heart started pounding. He'd snuck up on her and she'd never even noticed. Fates, he was good.

"I didn't think I would either," she told him, standing up on her toes so she could practically yell into his ear.

The music was loud and the forced closeness was strange after being so careful for so long.

Lucien looked her up and down, gaze snagging on the bone bracelet before meeting her eyes again. "Would you like a tour, little witch?"

Mika had to tear her eyes from his and looked over to Audrey who was watching them with a smirk. Her dorm mate raised an eyebrow in question and tapped her nose. Mika glared and shook her head. Lucien would definitely not be the one.

The hunter glanced over at Audrey, smiling slightly. "That's your friend right? She watched our first class."

Mika nodded. "Yeah, I came here with her tonight. So thank you for the offer, but I'm not leaving her."

"Well then," Lucien said, slipping his hands into the pockets of his leather pants. "She's welcome to join."

Blinking, Mika tried to decipher if there was some hidden meaning in those words.

"It's okay, go with him," Audrey said, leaning forward to practically yell into Mika's ear. "There's a hunter over there I want to ask to dance."

Mika looked over at the girl pouring herself a drink from the keg. She was cute. "Don't drink anything you don't recognize," Mika told her. "Enchanted drinks aren't always kind. If it doesn't look enchanted do a reveal spell anyway. And for the love of Artemis don't let hunters talk you into their deadly games."

Audrey just laughed and kissed her cheek. "I'll be fine. Go have fun."

Her dorm mate wove through the crowd of people –

there were already tons of students – and made her way to the hunter.

Then it was just her and Lucien. Mika looked up at him and resisted sighing.

She just wanted to get through her freshman year without killing anyone.

And somehow—somehow the universe knew it and was testing her. Lucien and Ethan were the ultimate distractions and Mika wasn't impervious to their good looks.

Those leather pants and Lucien's hazel brown eyes. Fuck. The way his nearly shoulder-length black hair fell into his face made her knees weak.

"I'm not looking for anything serious," she warned him. "I don't want a boyfriend."

Lucien's grin widened until she could see his canines – unusually sharp. Did he get them sharpened? Mika had heard some hunters did that to intimidate and confuse their prey.

"I'm not asking you to go steady," Lucien murmured. She could still hear him despite the music and it made her shiver. "Just asking if you'd like to see the infamous hunter house. Did you know it's haunted?"

She didn't know that. "Just wanted to make that clear." Mika waved her hand at the house. "I'd love a tour."

He didn't offer her his arm, and Mika was grateful. She didn't need help walking. But Lucien still stayed close enough that it drew attention from anyone they passed. He headed right for the stairs and then waited at the bottom for her to go up first.

Mika glared as she tried to decide if he wanted her to go up first so he could look up her skirt.

"If you fall, I'm here to catch you," Lucien said with a wink. "No other reason."

Right.

Mika grumbled. She was *not* clumsy.

The stairs were just like the ones in Oleander House but the outside wall wasn't made of glass. This entire house was made from thick wood. It reminded her of a posh cabin in the woods rather than the gothic stone houses the witches used.

When she reached the second floor Mika stepped to the side to let Lucien pass. He flashed another grin at her. "The main floor is a bit crowded right now," he told her, walking leisurely down the hall. "But that's where our living room is, where the kitchen, common area, study areas, and gym are. We are very lucky we get the biggest dorm on the island."

Mika felt like Lucien was being sarcastic, but she didn't say anything.

She kept her eyes between his shoulder blades to keep them off of his ass in those tight leather pants. And here she'd thought *he* would be the one ogling her. For some reason she felt like he knew she was staring.

Lucien was a hunter which meant he was massive and ripped and just...built to make her weak in the knees. He stopped at the window at the end of the hall and looked outside where the party was just as crazy.

They'd only had two classes together so far, but Mika knew just from his fighting style that he was aggressive and...patient. He played the long game and constantly pushed her to do better. When they weren't paired Mika could feel his eyes on her and still he never lost a match.

Except that one time she'd disarmed him.

"This house used to be the original school," Lucien told her. "Or it was before there was money involved and more than a hundred students anyway. One year a spell went wrong." He looked at her again and his hazel eyes looked lighter – nearly a honey color. "They say forty-nine witches died."

Forty-nine...

A chill went down Mika's spine. Seven sets of seven – a holy number to witches and they were just...massacred.

"Sometimes on a full moon you can see them out there in the trees," Lucien murmured, pointing to the forest just beyond the clearing for the house.

Mika looked up to see that, thankfully, it wasn't a full moon.

She knew the phases of the moon deep in her soul like most witches did, but Lucien's story had her doubting and on edge. "They didn't cleanse the space?" she asked. "They didn't put those witches' souls to rest?"

The smile on his face was gone and Lucien studied her closer. "It happened a long time ago. No one really knows what spell killed those witches or how. But they say it has something to do with the seven seals to hell. Rumor has it there's one under the school."

Her blood chilled and Mika took a step back. She

didn't bother to question how or why Lucien knew this. He was older which meant he'd been here longer. Students talked and this branch of the University of Morgana was old – older than Harvard even if it was only by a decade or two.

Mika didn't doubt that Lucien was telling the truth, and thinking of what could have possibly killed *forty-nine* witches chilled her to the bone.

She turned to leave, but Lucien was faster than she was. His hand snaked out and wrapped around her right wrist – the bare one. He eyed the rings she'd moved to that hand and then tugged her forward.

It wasn't enough to press her against him, but she could feel his body heat warming her skin. "Why does that scare you?" Lucien asked. His voice was deep and soothing, telling her that he would make sure she was safe.

It calmed her even though Mika didn't trust it. "Seven sets of seven," she murmured, shaking her head. "I don't want to know what happened to cause that."

"You can't just bury your head in the sand every time you come across something you don't like," Lucien told her, grip tightening on her wrist. It didn't hurt, but she knew it could if he wanted. "You avoid everything you don't like or understand. How is that healthy?"

Mika yanked her hand out of his grip and glared, knowing the only reason she could was because he let her. "I never pretended it was."

That confession made Lucien tilt his head and narrow his eyes at her. "Why are you taking a hunter class?" He took her hand again, but this time it was gentle. Slowly he pulled her forward until she was pressed up against his chest and Mika was so discombobulated by him she didn't even resist.

"Maybe I want to be a hunter," she breathed, feeling her heart pounding and wondering if he could feel it too with the way they were pressed together.

Lucien reached up and held her face, thumb gently caressing her cheek. "If that were true you'd be living here," he murmured.

The way he looked into her eyes...fucking *fuck* she was in trouble. "I'm undeclared – trying to find what I enjoy the most."

He smiled at that but didn't bother calling her out on the lie they both knew it was. Lucien bent down and kissed her anyways. Mika felt like the breath was sucked right out of her body.

This was nothing like kissing Ethan.

Lucien was electric and dark and full of anger. She didn't understand it, but it felt like he was taking that anger out on her with the way he nipped her bottom lip and gripped her lower back hard enough Mika knew she would have bruises there in the morning.

But it didn't scare her or turn her off. It actually did the opposite. She groaned into his mouth when his tongue flicked across her lips. Lucien made her lose her mind and suddenly she had her arms wrapped around his neck, hands buried in that silky black hair of his, using it to yank him down when he tried to pull away.

Mika refused to let him be the one in total control.

She kissed him back, sliding her tongue into his mouth as she pressed her entire body against his. When he was breathing just as hard as she was, hands gripping her hips like she might disappear if he let her go…

She pushed him away, watching as his chest heaved. Mika glared at him, but didn't say anything.

"That was wildly inappropriate." Her quiet words only seemed to make him angrier.

His eyes flashed and Lucien gripped her wrist, the one with the bone bracelet. "Why do you smell like blood?" he hissed. "What are you hiding, little witch?"

Mika gasped when his honey-colored eyes turned molten and glowed gold.

Lucien was a shifter.

21

Lucien's eyes were glowing *gold*.

Just like a cat shifter's.

"I'll tell you my secret if you tell me yours," Mika whispered.

Instantly Lucien released her and blinked. Just like that his eyes were a hazel brown, lighter than most Korean's but not something that really stood out if you didn't know.

"Hm, I don't know if I like that game," Lucien said, slipping his hands back into his pockets. He started walking back towards the stairs. "But I'll figure your secret out eventually," he said.

Mika was outraged. She gritted her teeth and stomped over to him, grabbing his arm and yanking him around. "How dare you?"

"Dare I do what?" Lucien asked, one eyebrow raised at her like she was just some nobody bothering him.

"Kiss me like that and then just...just leave!"

"I thought you didn't want anything serious?" Lucien smiled at her and she could have sworn there was a flash of gold.

"Mika, is everything okay?"

Instantly she released the shifter and glared at Ethan. "It's fine."

"See you in class, Mika," Lucien called over his shoulder as he headed down the stairs.

So much for a tour. He'd just wanted to know why she smelled like blood. Mika bared her teeth at Lucien's back in annoyance.

Which meant he could smell blood magic.

If he had been able to smell it earlier she was pretty sure he would have mentioned it when they were sparring – so it must be the bone bracelet. Was that a shifter skill, or somehow specific to him?

"Are you sure?" Ethan asked, turning to watch Lucien go with a carefully blank expression. "Looked like an argument to me."

"I said it was fine, Ethan." Mika whirled back to the window and crossed her arms over her chest. Was it too early to leave the party? The last thing she needed right now was to explain to Ethan why she was kissing Lucien, or wonder if he'd seen them.

This was why she didn't want to get involved with boys. Mika didn't want to have to deal with them or choose one when both satisfied very different needs...

Kenzie had three foxes and each was completely different. Mika was starting to understand why three mates worked so well.

Being loyal to one seemed like a terrible idea. How was she going to find out what she really needed that way, or if she was missing out on something else?

Nothing serious...who was she kidding?

"Why are you in a hunter class?" Ethan asked, leaning against the wall next to the window so he could study her face. "I didn't know you were entertaining that as a career choice."

"You didn't know that because we just met," Mika told him. "We barely know each other."

"Ouch." Ethan's eyebrows rose up nearly into his hairline. "Excuse the fuck out of me, but yeah you're right. It hasn't been that long."

They stood there in silence, watching the band set up.

"Do you want me to back off?" he asked softly, the irritation leaving his eyes. "It seems like you and Lucien have...a thing."

Mika sighed, feeling the anger drain out of her. Of course Ethan wouldn't be all macho and pushy and demand she choose him over the hunter. Glancing at him, she nearly broke down and cried from the overload of emotions.

Why did this all have to be so hard?

"Yes." Mika threw up her hands. "No." It was just the first week and she was already more confused than she was before she arrived. "I don't know," she admitted. "I don't know what I want, but I like you Ethan. A lot."

He looked down and his eyes widened when he saw

her hands were bare. "I like you a lot too, Mika. So…let's just take things slow, yeah? Nothing exclusive."

Mika was shocked. "Are you serious?"

Ethan shrugged and smiled down at the bone bracelet. "I'm not going to pretend I could satisfy your every need. Is that bracelet new?"

Looking down at the creepy piece of jewelry that kept her from killing Lucien the same way she'd nearly killed Ethan, Mika wondered if that was something they could really do. Could they have an open relationship and make it work?

Humans did that shit all the time.

And witches didn't wed back before they'd integrated into human society – no man could own them if they never married and had no fathers. But they had men they were with – for love, for sex, and to reproduce.

"Audrey and I found a binding spell," Mika told him. She lifted up the hand covered in silver bones and flexed it. Somehow the bones looked almost real. "I used a blood magic spell. It works too, tested it and everything."

"Really?" Ethan reached out and placed his hand against hers, fingertips to fingertips. "This is amazing. But doesn't this make it so you can't do magic at all?"

It was so weird to touch his skin and know she couldn't hurt him. "Yup. That's the catch."

Ethan laced his fingers through hers. "And what about the block and all that?"

Mika shrugged. "Why do you care?"

He tapped her nose and smiled. "Because you're an

amazing witch. It would be a shame to see all that power and skill go to waste because you're afraid."

She yanked her hand out of his and glared.

These boys were calling her out and Mika didn't like it. "I'm allowed to be afraid," she told him. "I killed someone and didn't mean it. Imagine what I could do if I tried?"

Mika turned and stalked toward the stairs.

She was going to find Audrey and tell her she was calling it quits for the night. Her boots made enough noise on the stairs as she stomped down to draw attention on any normal night, but the music was blasting and the band had officially started up.

It wasn't just the fear of her power that was causing the block. Mika knew what power felt like—what amped up power felt like. And blood magic was a thousand times worse. It could be addicting and tempting.

How easy would it be to do a spell that required a human's life as the sacrifice instead of a little bit of her own blood?

Granted there wasn't a lot she really knew about blood magic. She'd only made it a few chapters into some of the books Eisheth had suggested. It was difficult to digest when everything talked about using blood from people like it was no big deal.

Mika had grown up with snooty witches. They were judgy and turned up their nose at what some of them considered 'kitchen magic' or something like that. Necromancy and blood magic were talked about only in hushed whispers.

It was a dark magic – and somehow Mika could use it without even trying.

Someone had died and it had been an accident.

Her power terrified her – whispered horror stories as teens about the things some of the dark magics could do…

Mika shivered and practically ran the rest of the way down the stairs.

She crashed into someone at the bottom of the stairs and muttered an apology for not paying attention. She needed to get out of here.

"Whoa, are you okay?" Malachi steadied her and peered down like she might just pass out or something.

"I'm fine," Mika told him. "I haven't had anything to drink." She pushed off his hands and scanned the room for Audrey.

Where the hell was that girl?

"I saw Audrey with Natalie out there," Malachi said carefully, tilting his head toward the massive backyard. "I'm sorry."

Mika glared up at him. "I'm not gay and she's not my girlfriend."

Malachi blinked and then he smiled. "Is that right?"

Definitely time to leave.

"Just tell her I went home." Mika turned to leave, ignoring the way he smiled at her.

Malachi was a large dude. It took everything she had not to look at his arms in that short-sleeved shirt or how his dark skin practically glowed under the warm lights.

"Hey," Malachi called. "Are you sure everything's okay?"

Mika stopped and glanced over her shoulder at him. She looked the dodgeball captain up and down. "You're friends with Audrey right?"

He nodded.

"Make sure she gets home safe and at a decent time. She has tryouts tomorrow." Mika headed toward the door with every intention of having a long-ass bubble bath.

Then a scream pierced the air.

22

M ika froze as everything seemed to stop.

That scream had sounded like Audrey.

Another scream and she was running, shoving Malachi aside, pushing past random party-goers.

She shouldn't have left Audrey's side. The girl was basically a baby witch. She'd never lived in the paranormal world and born witches didn't want to educate her – they wanted to torture her.

Mika shoved another student and another until she found the source of the screaming.

Audrey was on the ground, holding her head like it might explode with the pretty hunter trying to hold her, to keep her from hurting herself.

"Move," Mika snapped—shoving some random. She ran to Audrey's side and dropped to her knees, checking her temperature and pupils. "What happened?"

"I don't know," Natalie said. "One minute we were dancing and the next she collapsed."

"I thought you were a hunter," Mika demanded. "Isn't it your damn job to protect people?"

She didn't bother waiting for a response. Mika ripped off her bracelet and bit her thumb hard enough to draw blood. A simple word as she waved her hand over Audrey's head told her what it was.

"Mika!" Ethan sounded just as panicked as she felt as he shoved through the crowd toward her.

"I need jewelweed!" Mika begged Ethan with her eyes. "Please." They didn't have time for her to apologize and she didn't know a spell she could do with blood magic or offensive magic that would heal Audrey. "Hurry."

Ethan knelt down next to her without hesitation and pulled a long necklace out of his shirt. He opened the large locket and selected a plant. "This should be enough for whatever she ingested."

Mika implored him without words, asking him to understand what she needed.

Ethan nodded and spoke the word that would turn the plant into a cure-all – as a natural antidote it had healing properties laced into its DNA. All it took was a little magic to make it more potent.

She held Audrey still so he could feed her the plant; Mika wrapped one leg around Audrey's in a hold to keep her from thrashing free. The strain of keeping her still eased and Mika looked up to see Lucien holding Audrey's legs.

The shifter nodded – all trace of games had disappeared from his face when she'd needed help.

Then Malachi was pushing back the crowd of people surrounding them, asking people to give them space, asking if anyone had seen anything, and generally calming people down.

Mika closed her eyes and said a quick prayer as she shoved the weed into Audrey's mouth. She hoped they'd been fast enough.

Then she concentrated on keeping her magic under control. Because if she didn't...Audrey could die a worse death than this.

Her dorm mate opened her eyes and gasped, back arching so far Mika was afraid it would snap.

"Hey, you're okay," Mika told her, brushing Audrey's hair back from her face and checking her pupils again. "You're okay. It was just a spell."

Audrey turned and hugged Natalie – the hunter cried with relief as she held the witch.

This wasn't over – Mika wasn't done. "Who slipped her that spell?" she asked, making sure everyone could hear her.

Without the music there was utter silence. Mika glared at the ones still staring, trying to find a guilty face.

"Who poisoned her?" Mika demanded, standing up and taking a step toward the crowd. "A hallucinogenic spell like that can kill someone. This isn't a fucking game."

"She's not a witch," Crystal said, stepping out from the crowd. "She doesn't belong here."

"Mika, don't," Lucien warned. Somehow he already

knew and was moving toward her, but rage made her faster than him just this once.

There were no sigils or runes to draw, no words to speak. Without her bracelet her power was there and ready. It blasted out of her just like it had in the greenhouse, but this time it was focused with her rage.

Crystal went flying across the yard.

The sound of her landing in the snow was loud in the silence and her pitiful cry of pain only made Mika want to hear her *scream* just like Audrey had.

Mika stalked toward Crystal, not finished with her yet. This mean girl who wanted to torture others deserved to suffer for what she'd done to Audrey – for everything poisoning her meant, and for the way too many witches were looking away from Mika in shame and guilt.

This had to stop.

Now.

"Hey, don't," Lucien warned, grabbing her. "You don't want to get expelled."

Mika whipped around and snarled at him. "I don't care. Not if it keeps Crystal and others like her from doing that to anyone else ever again."

"Be smart," he hissed.

She was so furious all she could see was red. Mika swung and Lucien wasn't expecting the physical attack. Her punch landed and his head whipped to the side. The look of shock on his face almost snapped her out of it.

"I'm bleeding," he said in complete surprise, pressing a finger to his nose. "Holy shit, little witch. Nice job."

"Looks like you gotta try out tomorrow," Audrey croaked.

Mika turned to the only friend she had in the world and wrapped her arms around her, helping Audrey to her feet. The rest of her anger leaked away as she focused on Audrey. "You know it doesn't count," she grumbled, fixing her dark hair.

"A nose bleed is a nose bleed babe, and you caused it." If she hadn't almost died Mika would wipe that smirk right off Audrey's face.

"Someone lock Crystal up before I do," Mika said, taking some of Audrey's weight. "We'll be reporting her in the morning."

Ethan handed her the bone bracelet with a pointed look and Mika took it with a quiet thank you. Just touching the silver had that weight settling over her like a blanket. Mika slipped on the bracelet as quickly as she could.

Each second Audrey was in skin to skin contact with her was a risk. Mika fumbled to put it on and still hold up the other witch.

"Let me help." Malachi swept Audrey into his arms and cradled her against his chest. "I'll help you get her back to your dorm."

"And I'll get a spell to restore her to full strength," Ethan murmured, disappearing into the crowd like a phantom.

Then it was just Mika and everyone who was staring at her.

She couldn't hide anymore. They'd all seen the power she could wield if she chose to.

So, what now?

"You smell like blood, little witch," Lucien whispered, brushing his arm against her shoulder. This time though, his words were gentle.

Mika looked up at the hunter and even though his eyes weren't glowing she knew they could. "Your eyes are so pretty, hunter. I'm almost jealous."

That made Lucien smile. They both knew she could never get eyes like his.

Mika followed after Malachi and Audrey then, glancing back only once at Crystal. Natalie already had her cuffed and no doubt had her magic bound. The hunter hauled the snotty bitch to her feet and shoved her towards one of the buildings outside.

She didn't want to know and she had no plans to ask. But as soon as the office was open, Mika was going to report the bitch for a hate crime. Hopefully it was enough to get her expelled.

All this was against everything she'd sworn not to do. Don't get involved, don't draw attention to herself – and don't get attached. It was only the first week and she'd broken every single one of those rules.

Guess Mika couldn't stand on the sidelines anymore.

Her favorite sun room was empty again. It helped it was smaller than some of the others which left room for only two tables, aside from the plants and a little sitting area. For a room meant to let in light it was grey and dark this early in the morning.

The cloud cover didn't help either.

Mika couldn't stop sneaking glances at Audrey as they ate in silence.

"If you don't stop I'm going to stab you with my fork," Audrey muttered, taking another bite of her breakfast burrito. She was one of those weirdos who ate burritos with forks.

"How are you feeling?" Mika asked, fiddling with her spoon. Reporting Crystal this morning had been as easy as filing a report. Now they had to wait and see what the school board would do.

"Other than tired, I'm doing great thanks to that tonic or whatever it was Ethan gave me." Audrey gave her a pointed look. "I'll be even better when I finish this energy drink."

"I have no idea how you can drink that crap this early in the morning," Mika muttered, sipping at her coffee.

They'd gone to bed late so they were both cranky. Mika had managed to refrain from saying 'I told you so' though, so she was counting that as a personal win.

Malachi had hovered after carrying Audrey home, making sure she was tucked into bed and that the potion Ethan had given her worked. Mika had to give him props for not once hitting on her or flirting with her while he took care of Audrey.

Those two were actual friends who seemed closer than Mika had originally thought. Watching them had been like looking into an alternate world – but she assumed the fall semester was when they'd gotten close.

The captain of the Morgana Marauders was actually as nice as he seemed – a man who you could always count on, who would always have your back, and who would always drop everything to help his friends out – to help out anyone who was in a less advantageous situation.

Malachi would be a superhero if there was such a thing.

Then he'd sat there in the overstuffed velvet chair next to Audrey's bed until she'd fallen asleep.

Mika took a bite of oatmeal as she remembered that hushed conversation with him while her friend snored.

The jock knew about the issues with the natural born witches versus the human ones and that was why he'd befriended Audrey at the beginning of her freshman year despite him being two years older.

Mika hadn't said anything to that, but she was impressed and also...touched.

There were some good guys still out there. It was just that it never felt like there were enough of them.

The sun poked through the clouds and Mika looked up at the glass ceiling as the sunlight filled the room. Maybe it wouldn't be a gloomy day after all.

"Could you tell Ethan thank you?" Audrey said for the hundredth time. She drained her energy drink and set the can on the table with a clink. "That potion did some serious magic on me."

Mika nodded, not bothering to remind Audrey she'd already thanked Ethan about a dozen times in person the night before.

She flushed remembering the way he'd stuck around after giving Audrey the potion. Mika had been too flustered to tell him to leave, or to kick out Malachi – especially when that one hadn't been there for Mika.

But Ethan saw too much. Even from day one he'd seen right through her. There was something about him that was just...perceptive as hell.

One look at Malachi and Ethan had given her a smirk.

Mika had no feelings for the captain, but she would never deny she was attracted to him.

Sighing, she drained her coffee and poured more from the French press that always stayed hot thanks to the enchantment on the silver.

Ethan had kissed her goodnight once Audrey had felt normal again and had left Oleander House – giving her the space she hadn't even realized she'd needed. It never ceased to surprise her how attuned Ethan was to her.

He hadn't deserved what she'd said to him at the party.

She knew she was a fucking mess. Mika spent most of her time and energy dealing with all the shit that had fallen into her lap three years ago. Finding a little extra to be pleasant to people was...exhausting.

So most of the time she didn't even bother.

But for Ethan...he deserved an apology, and for her to try harder.

"Are you ready for tryouts?" Audrey asked, finishing her burrito. The other witch eyed the bone bracelet still on Mika's hand suspiciously. "You're not going to back out of the deal are you?"

Mika shook her head. "I never go back on my word."

It still was the worst idea ever. If someone ended up hurt or dead...that would be on her – not Audrey.

"So...are you as excited as I am?" Audrey tapped the stone table over and over, adjusting the gear she'd bought last semester.

Mika just wore the outfit she wore to her hunter class since she hadn't had time to buy anything. It wasn't as protective, but that was fine. Audrey had spelled it with the same shit that was in the normal gear. But Mika wasn't actually worried about getting hurt.

Audrey wanted to try out as a matching set. They were going to work as a team during tryouts.

Ironically Audrey had been the first one up after all that had happened the night before, making Mika get dressed so they could practice strategies as a duo.

It was only nine in the morning and she'd been up for hours.

She should have just pulled an all-nighter – can't wake up tired if she never slept to begin with.

"I can see you're so excited you can barely contain it," Audrey said sarcastically. "Come on; let's get over to the stadium. It's going to be crowded and I don't want to be late."

"That many people huh?" Mika asked as she grabbed her dishes.

"Since this is the first time this year's freshman students have had a chance to try out, uh yeah. Everyone and their mom is going to be there," Audrey snorted. She followed after Mika with the French press and her empty plate.

Great, so practically the entire school was going to show up – and then whoever wanted to just watch since anyone could cheer on the intended hopefuls.

They would all be watching Mika and if she accidentally fucked up...

It would be fine. She was working with Audrey and that would help. Then her gear covered her from her neck down. Fingerless gloves would make it easier to cast magic while limiting the amount of skin exposed.

Mika washed her dishes and tried to convince herself this was going to be okay. It wasn't going to go badly even though every tiny thing that could go wrong played in her head like a morbid picture wheel slathered in blood.

They went up to their room in silence. For once Audrey didn't try to fill it with her chatter. She must be nervous as well then. Mika couldn't remember the last time her dorm mate hadn't talked just to talk.

Pushing open their door, Mika stopped dead when she saw who was standing in their room.

This day just kept getting better and better.

UNIVERSITY OF MORGANA

How the hell had he even gotten into their bedroom?

The fox was eyeing the makeup on their vanity, hands clasped behind his back.

"What are you doing here, Hunter?" Mika demanded.

Audrey shoved past Mika so she could see what was going on.

"I told you I'd be by," he reminded her. "You should lock your windows."

"It's the third floor," she snapped.

He just gave her a look that said '*I got in here, didn't I?*' and Mika wanted to rake it off his face with her nails.

"Definitely locking the window now," Audrey muttered, crossing the room to her armoire. "I do *not* want to wake up with *you* hovering over me."

"Kenzie, Selene, Finnick, and Ash are getting coffee and donuts," Hunter said, ignoring Audrey's whispered jab. "They'll meet us at the stadium. I came here first to give you these."

That's when Mika noticed the stack of books on the vanity. They looked pretty new considering.

"What are those?" Mika asked, going to her armoire to find what she needed.

"Books on anything I thought you could use," Hunter said quietly, watching as she grabbed her gloves and coat, eyes zeroing in on the bone bracelet she wore. "Something happened last night."

Audrey stared at him in disbelief. "How could you possibly know that?"

"Foxes can sense pain," Mika murmured, remembering what Hunter had told her. "It's none of your business, Hunter. No one died."

He smirked at that. "Unfortunate, but seeing as how death bothers you I'm grateful for your sake."

Death didn't really bother her, but when it was an innocent?

Mika contemplated that thought for a second and then yanked on her coat.

"I got you books on blood magic, on the university itself that not even the original University of Morgana possesses – since it was established before witches were neutral and they don't like remembering that – books on battle magic no longer in circulation, and then just one that I found concerning magical blocks."

Her scarf slipped from her fingers and Mika just gaped at Hunter. "I don't understand."

The way he shrugged like it was no big deal grated

on her nerves. "Before witches were in charge of the lore and the archives, foxes were. There is a lot in our libraries that witches purged or tried to hide. But the fox libraries are hidden and protected. Don't worry; these are copies and gifts from me to you. I advise that you enchant the covers like you did on the others though."

Just like that he slipped his hands in his pockets and walked toward the door – not the window, thank the Fates.

"Wait...what?" For some reason Mika couldn't process his words.

Hunter stopped and looked at her over his shoulder, one eyebrow raised. "It was a long time ago."

There was so much in his simple statement that Mika couldn't unpack at the moment. She shook her head and decided she'd have to ask him a thousand questions later. Wrapping her scarf around her neck she fell into step beside Audrey and picked up her pace.

Mika didn't want to be late.

"So why bring books on the university?" Audrey asked. "Is there something about this place they don't want us to know about?"

"There's always something," Hunter said, taking the stairs two at a time just ahead of them. "It would be best to know what that something is if you're going to be living here for five years and hiding your specialty from them."

Mika really didn't like the sound of that.

As if she didn't have enough homework, there were all those books too.

"Did you find anything useful on the other stuff?" Audrey asked carefully, linking her arm in Mika's.

Hunter eyed the empty common rooms on the bottom floor and then opened the main door for them. "I did."

Audrey rolled her eyes and Mika was tempted to do the same. Why did Hunter have to drag everything out all the time?

"So?" the other witch asked. "What did you find?"

"There have been specialties in this before," Hunter said carefully, looking around to make sure no one could overhear them.

He was the only one who seemed to be aware of how controversial this was, which Mika was grateful for.

The snow crunched under their boots as they walked across the freshly fallen snow from the night before. The paths looked slick this early and Mika wasn't interested in getting an injury before tryouts.

Hunter walked beside them, slightly apart, constantly looking around, but everyone was either asleep, or at the stadium. "It's unusual to have this as a specialty," he said. "But not as rare as a void witch. Most of what I found was before witches became neutral. Anything after that is carefully worded. You'll have to decipher what you can from it."

The trees started to get thicker and thicker as they entered the mini forest on the five hundred acre island. On the other side was the stadium and Mika felt her adrenaline spike. She was actually nervous.

What if she didn't make the team?

"Were they all evil?" Mika asked, looking up at the sky. It was actually sunny out for the first time since she'd arrived at the university.

"A lot, but not all," Hunter murmured. "It's just like being a void from what I saw. The magic itself is neutral. What you do with it is up to you."

Mika sighed. It was an answer, but not really.

Glancing down at the silver peeking out from her glove, she wondered what a blood specialty could even do if it wasn't to kill. Perhaps there would be some answers in necromancy which was a bit more common and just as controversial.

They didn't even offer necromancy as a specialty at the university anymore.

"Hunter." Mika slid off her left glove and started taking off her bracelet. "Did you know that the original building used for the university now houses the hunters?"

He eyed her but didn't say anything.

"One of the hunters told me it was haunted," she said, removing the rings. "That a long time ago something bad happened – no one knows exactly what – and forty-nine witches died."

Instantly he stopped and gave her a sharp look. "Forty-nine?"

A chill ran down her spine and Audrey shivered next to her.

The adrenaline in Mika's blood called to her magic and she felt it rising steadily – less forceful this time. It was like it somehow knew what she had planned for it and didn't want to waste a drop of power.

"Doesn't sound like an accident," Hunter mused. Then he started walking again, faster this time.

Audrey and Mika rushed to catch up. "It was," Audrey insisted. "I heard the story. A spell went wrong and those witches died horrible, excruciating deaths that no one could have planned for."

The trees started to thin and Mika was almost hot with the sun shining down on them. Just beyond the tree line she could make out the gothic stadium rising up from the ground like some behemoth.

"No, it wasn't an accident," Hunter insisted. He started scanning the small groups of people as they got closer, and his pace unconsciously picked up.

"Then what was it?" Mika snapped, practically jogging to keep up with him.

"There they are." Hunter stopped just at the end of the forest, one step before the space was completely clear of anything but decorative trees. "It's not an accident because seven sets of seven is a number too perfect for witches. If I was a betting fox, I'd put a thousand dollars on it being some kind of blood spell."

"But why?" Mika asked. She shivered as gruesome images tried to infiltrate her thoughts.

The fox shrugged. "That's the real question, isn't it?"

"We got you guys donuts too," Selene said with that pretty smile of hers, handing a box to Mika as they got closer. "I hope you like glazed."

Mika flexed her hand. It felt bare without the bone bracelet. "You didn't have to do that," she quietly told Selene.

It had been a long time since she'd spent *any* time with Selene. Trolling under the radar meant she couldn't really be friends with a matriarch even if Selene had the time to hang out with her. Not to mention all the other complications.

Their lives couldn't be more different.

Selene had to grow up fast and even though they were both nineteen, Mika felt like she was years younger as she studied the posh woman in front of her. "What are you doing here?" Mika asked.

"Kenzie told me Hunter had a few things to drop off.

That he was...mentoring you." Selene tilted her head slightly as she looked Mika up and down.

The way Selene studied her reminded Mika a lot of Kenzie.

"Thank you again for keeping them entertained," Kenzie snorted, sipping her coffee. "But had I known I would have to come here at the crack ass of dawn I would have found another babysitter."

"It's battle magic!" Finnick said, bumping fists with Audrey. "I wouldn't miss this for the world whether Hunter wanted to play teacher or not."

Audrey hugged Ash, and Kenzie started asking Mika's dorm mate about their strategy, giving her and Selene the illusion of privacy.

"So, why did you really come?" Mika asked, tucking her hands into her coat pockets.

Selene smiled slightly and opened the box of donuts. "To be honest I was curious more than anything. Kenzie said you had tryouts today and Hunter was talking about the books he'd gotten for you." She shrugged and looked down at the donuts. Mika took one just so she would stop offering. "Then I realized how much we've grown apart, and the last time I really talked to you was years ago...I feel like a shitty friend."

Finding the right words wouldn't be easy. There was a lot to detangle from this mess.

"You had a lot going on," Mika finally said, shrugging. She took a bite out of the donut and enjoyed the way it practically dissolved on her tongue, tasting of butter and sugar. "You're the youngest matriarch in the coven and brilliant. Duty calls and all that."

Selene looked away, studying the stadium. "Yes and no. I should have noticed something was different with you. We were still in school together when...that happened."

Mika glared at the foxes and Kenzie, but no one would look at her directly. "So you know everything then."

"Yeah, I do," Selene admitted, tucking the box of donuts into her bag. "It's...I'm sorry. I should have been there for you."

They stood there awkwardly and Mika felt her heart clench as she fought off tears. "I never blamed you," she whispered. "And I'm so, so sorry I didn't tell you about him. It wasn't just your fault. I didn't know how to be friends with you and keep this shitty secret."

Selene's voice was hard when she said, "I knew who he was which is why I dissolved our engagement the second I became matriarch, but I didn't know he'd hurt others."

Mika studied Selene then and realized even if the other witch had been a virgin for her contract, that didn't mean Bradley Davis had never hurt her. "We need to remind ourselves and the others that witches have been warriors since the dawn of our race. Somewhere along the way, we've forgotten."

They'd let the world and this hoity-toity society make them soft, make them weak. And the men had taken advantage.

Selene's dark blue eyes sparkled at that. "Sounds like you have something in mind."

She did actually. "Outlaw betrothals in our coven as a start when you become High Priestess," Mika told her, crossing her arms over her chest. How she reacted to this would definitely show Mika what kind of witch Selene really was. "With your position and power you can petition the Council of Paranormals to outlaw it completely before the age of sixteen, and only with the consent of the witch."

Selene grinned at that. "It would be my pleasure – *if* I make high priestess. But there are other ways. Upsetting the current regime sounds like my new favorite hobby."

"Really?" Mika asked, arms falling to her sides. "Then...would you help me find a way to allow shifters into this school? Any paranormal actually?"

The others stopped talking and all three foxes stared at her.

"Why?" Selene asked, tilting her head. "They can't perform magic."

The tingling started in her palms this time and Mika clenched her hands into fists. "Because they're not allowed. All that does is drive the wedge between us deeper. Would you be hanging out with shifters at all if your sister wasn't mated to them?"

"Hey," Kenzie said, taking a step forward. "I don't disagree with you, but don't fucking talk to my sister like that."

Mika took a step back, and decided that she should have just kept her mouth shut. She'd asked for help from someone far more powerful than she'd ever be – when the real question she should have asked was, 'would you still accept me into the coven knowing my specialty?'

Why didn't she just ask that?

Mika didn't want to admit how scared she was to hear the answer.

"No, it's okay Kenzie," Selene said, reaching out as Mika took another step back.

"Er, don't touch her skin," Audrey warned.

Selene's hand wrapped around Mika's covered wrist and they studied each other for a moment – the last three years was like a weight hanging over the both of them.

"I was just curious," Selene said. "It's definitely not something I'm opposed to. Would you like to talk about it sometime over coffee? The portal to the school is always open if you have your student ID. Are you planning to visit home at all?"

Already Mika felt like this place, Oleander House and Morgana, was her home more than that empty mansion back in San Francisco. But she wanted to check on her grandmother in person.

"I am. I'll let you know when I plan to head back."

There was a commotion on the other side of the stadium wall and Mika and Audrey shared a look.

"Twenty more minutes until tryouts start, but we should go in," Audrey told her.

Selene released Mika and they headed into the stadium.

Well, at least that was a start. No doubt it was something that wouldn't happen overnight, but Mika had taken that first step toward fixing some of the shit that was bothering her, instead of just talking about it.

The endless stairs echoed hundreds of voices and Mika tuned them out as she tried to settle her thoughts. Part of her wished that Kenzie and her foxes hadn't come to the tryouts, and especially not with Selene. But the other part of her, that was slowly realizing just how lonely she'd been over the last few years, was ecstatic to have the support.

But, what if she didn't make the team?

That would be embarrassing.

"We got this," Audrey told her, nudging Mika's shoulder with hers. "Get out of your head already."

They went through one of the doors at the top and eyed the circular hall that went around the entire stadium. On game nights there would be shirts and sweaters, food and drink for sale. It would be a party. Today they had a few coffee carts, but that was it.

Audrey and Mika went through the door directly opposite the stairs and eyed the massive field below them.

More people were in the seats than she'd expected to see and Mika's stomach flip-flopped. Holy shit. A lot of people were going to be watching.

The last time she'd been here she'd nearly shoved Audrey right out of her life because of how terrified she was of her own power. She'd almost lost control of her magic because a handful of people were staring at her.

Compared to the people in the stadium seats this time – that had been nothing.

"It'll be fine," Audrey told her. "I won't let you fail."

Mika shot the other witch a grateful look.

In that moment it felt like neither of them would have made it through their freshman year without the other.

Had the Fates crossed their paths for a reason?

They took off their coats, gloves, and scarves. Mika handed hers to Hunter with a pointed look. "My bracelet better still be in there when I get back."

The alpha fox gave her a sharp grin and Mika almost snatched it back, but Audrey was staring at something.

"Your boy toys are sitting together." Audrey jerked her chin and Mika followed the direction over to Lucien and...Ethan.

Lucien and Ethan were sitting together, eating donuts out of a box with coffee in their hands, like they'd come here together.

What the fuck?

"I still think he's hot," Finnick said, slapping her on the shoulder. "Who's that other one?"

The last thing she wanted was for the foxes to go over there and start asking questions. Lucien was a shifter hiding in a school for witches. She didn't want the foxes anywhere near him.

"A hunter," Mika told him. "I'm going to say hi, mind your business."

Finnick grinned at that and Ash chuckled as he found seats for everyone and got them settled.

Mika told Audrey she'd be right back and then headed for Ethan and Lucien.

Why were they sitting together like chums?

"Hey," she said. "Didn't realize either of you cared about dodgeball."

Lucien gave her a sharp smile. "Didn't realize you were going to try out, little witch."

"She's fucking fantastic," Ethan said, smiling up at her. "You'll do great. Try not to kill anyone."

Mika narrowed her eyes at him, and then flicked a look at Lucien. "So, did you two come here together?"

"Maybe," Lucien said, smiling as he sipped his coffee. "But it's nothing serious."

Her cheeks felt like they were on fire and Mika didn't know what the fuck to say to that so she turned and stomped down the stairs toward the field.

Whatever games they were playing, she didn't have the time or energy to care at the moment.

"Hey, wait up!" Audrey called, jumping the stairs as she ran to catch up. "Are they here for you?"

"It doesn't matter," Mika told her. "We're here to try out for the team. Boys are a distraction I can't afford."

"*You're* a distraction," Audrey muttered, pointing at someone who was waving at them.

Mika found Ryan's clear blue eyes in the crowd. "You still owe me a muffin!" he called. Then he gave her a wink. "Good luck!"

Grabbing Audrey's arm she yanked her toward the field. "Let's just get this over with."

Malachi spotted them as they went down into the below-ground hall and punched in the code for the gate. It made an obnoxious noise as they entered the field.

Mika stomped across the bridge, practically dragging Audrey with her.

"Hey! You're trying out!" Malachi called as they took their places with the other freshmen.

"Don't say a fucking word," Mika muttered.

Audrey snickered. "Come on, Ms. Marshall. We have fans to entertain."

26

Now that they were on the field it felt like they were in a totally different world.

Mika looked up at the stadium seating around them, going higher and higher until it looked like the walls touched the clouds. But down here on the field was a little quieter. There was some chatter, but something about the way the field was built, how it was set into the ground, and the pool of water surrounding them buffered a lot of the noise.

Then there was the fact that the walls surrounding the field were slightly above them and suddenly it felt like the crowd was faceless. Mika couldn't find anyone she knew even if she'd tried.

Taking a moment to collect herself, she eyed the water. There was ice floating in it. If anyone went over... hopefully they had triage healers around.

"Hello!" Malachi said loud enough to startle Mika. His voice boomed in the dome-like structure and it was the first time she realized just how deep it was. "I'm the captain of the Morgana Marauders."

"Look," Audrey whispered. "Some of the professors came."

Mika didn't bother to look and see who. She didn't want to get more nervous than she already was. She ran through some of her best spells over and over again in her head, picturing the two-person strategy she and Audrey had decided on.

"The spring session will be eighty of us competing against each other for a spot on the university's main team for the coming fall," Malachi explained.

Two hundred potential Marauders on that field and Mika didn't doubt that every single one of them could hear him.

Malachi's dark skin shone in the sun and Mika had to tear her eyes away from the muscles in his arms. At least he was wearing a shirt this time.

"Some of you were on one of the teams last year and know how this goes. We're separated into team colors for spring. Now!" Malachi put his hands on his hips and stalked up and down the line of hopeful players. "We are going to run through normal practice routines. Some of you will be tapped on the shoulder before they're over. When that happens I ask that you leave right away. Those still here when practice is over will be separated and we'll start running scrimmages."

This was going to be brutal.

Mika was out of shape for something this intense. If

she made it through a college level practice, no doubt she'd barely be able to stand for the scrimmage.

"We'll be fine," Audrey whispered, more to herself than anything.

"I hate you," Mika muttered, crossing her arms over her chest to glare at nothing in particular. This was going to suck.

"You've trained to be a hunter," Audrey hissed. "Fucking deal with it."

They shouldn't have gone to that damn party. Both of them were cranky.

Mika was regretting the last six months she'd taken off after graduating. She should have kept up her hunter training, because if she couldn't get her magic under control it was either that or being a glorified gardener for her family's greenhouse.

"We're going to start with sprints!" Malachi stated cheerfully, as if this was his favorite part of practice.

No one dared groan though.

"The faster you are, the less likely you are to be hit! So, let's do this!" He chuckled as he started separating people into groups. "If it makes you feel better I'll be doing everything you are."

Of course he would. Mika begrudgingly admired him. Malachi was definitely some kind of all-American boy scout that you wanted to hate because he was so good at everything, but just too nice to really commit to that hate.

Then he was standing in front of her and Mika

blinked, hoping he couldn't tell just from her face that she'd been thinking about him.

"I'm glad you both decided to show up despite everything that happened last night," Malachi said, his voice quiet for the first time since she'd set foot on the field. "I've never seen you use battle magic, Mika, but after what I saw last night I was willing to beg you to join up."

The way he smiled down at her was disconcerting. Mika couldn't wipe the image of him on his knees before her.

Maybe she wanted him to beg.

Then he gave Audrey a playful punch on the shoulder and the spell was broken.

Mika cleared her throat awkwardly and followed him and Audrey to their places on the field. They all lined up on one of the sidelines and Mika suddenly realized just how big a university-sized field was. Playing this game was not going to be easy.

Malachi yelled across the field, "Are you ready?"

And suddenly the electric feel of adrenaline spiked through Mika like a lightning bolt. The excitement, desperation, and determination on the field was palpable as two hundred students made promises to themselves. They psyched themselves up and Mika knew everyone was going to give their best.

So she had to as well or she'd walk off this field as a disappointment, kicked out of another group she so desperately wanted to be a part of even if she would never admit it out loud. Mika didn't feel like she deserved to belong – to have fun like a normal witch.

Not after she'd killed someone.

But it had been an accident.

Maybe, just maybe she didn't deserve to suffer forever.

"Twenty sprints and go!" Malachi yelled.

Her body moved without her telling it to and Mika's muscles were still warm from her practice with Audrey at dawn. It felt good to be running – to be sprinting. To move her entire body as fast as it could go, stop on a dime, and then turn and just run hard—harder.

Limbs pumping, body moving, eye on Audrey...

Mika grinned as they hit the starting line and turned again.

Audrey was keeping pace with her, but could probably go faster if she wanted. Regardless they managed to be in the top twenty fastest runners.

It was just like riding a bike. Mika's body recognized this and knew what was coming next – what they were going to have to do for the next few hours. After all she'd played for years before she'd had to quit.

And her hunter instructors had been even more brutal in her training as she didn't have the super strength and speed a born hunter had.

By halfway her lungs were burning and her muscles were screaming, but this was just the beginning. They had to do whatever Malachi felt like torturing them with – to weed out the weak. And then they would have the actual battles.

Mika gritted her teeth and concentrated on each step, making sure Audrey didn't get too ahead of her.

Potential players were dropping from the tryouts like flies after they hit the thirteenth sprint and Mika wasn't going to lie to herself, she was seriously contemplating doing the same when she remembered she had *seven more to go*.

"Don't stop," Audrey told her. "We'll get a break after this and they're going to give us a little tonic. That's what Malachi said."

For some reason Malachi telling Audrey an insider secret so she could keep going...it pushed Mika to finish those last seven sprints even though her legs were burning and it felt like she would collapse if she stopped.

But they made it and the second her foot touched the line for the last time Mika dropped into a walk, hands on her hips, breathing hard. If she stopped walking her legs would stop working and if she fell, Mika highly doubted she'd be able to get up again.

Looked like she'd have to add runs to her daily schedule again. Fuck she hated running. It was her least favorite part of the hunter training, but her instructor had insisted she might have to run after a creature all night or *run away*.

The last one was what had motivated her.

A hunter could use charms to enhance speed and strength, but all that was illegal in battle magic dodgeball. So Mika had to be good, no – better than good. The only reassuring thing was that she was competing with a bunch of witches and not hunters.

For the first time she wasn't fucking last.

Someone shoved a cup in her hand and Mika drank the cool water gratefully. It had a slight citrus tang to it that was all that told her what kind of tonic it was. A healing tonic, thank the Fates.

The burning in her thighs eased and her breathing became less ragged. Mika downed the tonic-laced water. Another deep breath and she was almost back to normal.

"All right!" Malachi yelled, clapping. "Congrats to those who survived!"

That's basically what it felt like too – like she'd barely just survived.

"Good job," Audrey gasped, slapping her on the back. "Had I known we were doing suicides I would have trained you from the get-go. Didn't think you were going to make it."

"Me either."

Malachi started grouping people again and Mika stuck to Audrey's side and glared, daring him to separate them.

But he was a smart dude and didn't even try. He just directed the both of them over to a group that was going to start on the next physical activity – attacking the wooden dummies that were being brought out by some of the university staff.

Then it would be pushups.

Mika was more worried about the shielding aspect than she was about the pushups.

"Is there anything in the rules about shielding with

fire?" Mika muttered, getting into place behind Audrey. "I can't remember."

They moved up a spot as each player attacked once. Destroy the magical shield on the wooden dummy – if they couldn't damage it more than thirty percent they received the tap based on the amount of players who were already leaving the field.

Mika decided on a pure energy ball. It was the simplest form of attack, but also the most effective. If someone didn't shield right it was easy to knock them back with it.

How good was this shield spelled into a wooden opponent?

"The three approved shields are all defensive," Audrey muttered back, trying not to bring attention to them. "But fire is an approved attack along with the other elements. There's nothing that says you can't use an approved attack for defense. But it'll bring attention to you."

"If I try to use a normal shield I'm not going to make it," Mika told her. "I didn't realize we were going to be practicing like this. It's a lot easier to avoid shielding in a scrimmage."

"It'll be fine. Use fire, or the energy spell," Audrey told her, taking another step forward. "I don't think you'll get tapped."

Audrey was next and she looked back at Mika with a quirky smile. "If you do though, I'm still proud of you for climbing out of your little bubble to try."

The baby witch was patting her on the back and it

felt weird, like Mika was slow. But she actually was, thanks to her block.

She was only good at one thing.

Audrey got over sixty percent damage and Mika smiled slightly, proud of her. Then it was her turn.

Mika stepped forward and decided for the sake of full disclosure, she wasn't going to perform each step of the spell. She took a deep breath and it felt like the rest of the stadium did as well.

Everyone was definitely looking at her, she could feel it between her shoulders and her adrenaline was making her feel like she needed to move and fight and *do* something.

So she drew the sigil she'd created into the air that – combining the three required for this spell and didn't speak. She only thought the word she needed as she bent her knees and held up her hands.

Over and over she thought the word and cradled the ball of energy close to her chest as the power built with each thought of the word.

In a real game she would need to be able to run and dodge while doing this. Mika eyed the target and took one step forward, throwing the spell as hard as she could at the wooden player. Her spell ripped through the shield and disintegrated it – then the wooden player burst into a thousand splinters.

Everyone ducked but Mika had pulled her hands outward, thinking the word one last time as her fingers moved. The energy became a ring around the splinters, catching them before they could hurt anyone.

She dropped her hands then and the splinters fell to the ground harmlessly. Mika eyed those wooden pieces as she went to the back of the line and ignored Malachi's grin.

Destruction was the only thing she was really good at.

27

D estroying the dummy thankfully hadn't gotten her the tap. Mika had known it was a risk. Sometimes too much power scared people and they always wondered if it could be controlled. But Mika had learned something over the years about the only magic she could still do.

You couldn't control it like people wanted you to.

It was not a robot programmed with exact instructions that would never vary once the commands were known.

No, her magic was like a pitbull on the end of a leash. She'd raised it as a baby and it was a part of her – if she lost it she would always feel like something was missing. It was strong and powerful and followed commands.

But Mika could never forget her magic was never truly tame. It was born wild and free and even with practice and control and domestication there was always,

always a chance it would destroy something without meaning to.

If she stepped on a dog's tail – it didn't matter how well it was trained – it would bite her.

People would no doubt argue with her theory, saying service dogs didn't bite, that dogs didn't always bite, only more aggressive dogs would and the others would just whine in pain. But you could never really know which one it would be.

Aggressive magic was inherently defensive. A witch with a healing specialty would never hurt someone on purpose, but they could. Healing was a different form of aggression. The witch putting the bones back together could very easily shatter them apart too.

Only the witch controlling the magic had any real say over what was done with that power.

And Mika refused to be controlled by hers.

She still had to fight to keep it from destroying everything it touched, but she'd always locked it down – knowing her triggers and avoiding them.

Standing here on this field, knowing that she was purposefully using that aggressive magic prone to dark things – it terrified her. But it was also liberating. The magic was more acquiescent the more she used it.

Maybe she shouldn't have sequestered herself. Maybe she should have used it more.

But that didn't change how dangerous her odd specialty was. That was one of those things she couldn't really practice to control – not without getting every single council member on her case.

Blood magic.

What a fucking nightmare.

"All right, you're going to be shielding against a real attack!"

Thank goodness Malachi hadn't bothered trying to separate them. He must have seen. He must have inherently known they would work together or not at all. Though, Mika hoped if she got the tap that Audrey would stick it out.

She deserved to be on this team after all her hard work.

The girl was good too.

"I'll be careful," Audrey told her before heading across the field.

It would be tricky. Make it look like she was actually attacking as hard as she would if it was anyone else.

Mika could only shield with an attack, and thankfully they were allowed to retaliate. All the pairs would go back and forth until one of them was knocked off the field into the icy water, or the time was up.

Shielding for ten minutes didn't sound like a lot, but it would be a nightmare for Mika – no dodging allowed.

And she *really* didn't want to end up in the icy water.

This was definitely an easy way to weed out more people though, and the last test before they were divided up for scrimmages. After the first fifty people dropped out in the first hour it was one here and there instead of in droves.

Audrey attacked and Mika burned up the spell before retaliating.

She didn't use the same force as she did for that first attack on the dummy. That kind of strength she could use maybe once or twice in a game. It was her 'special' she supposed. Had to rebuild that kind of power back up before she could use it again.

They went back and forth – using close to full strength, but neither of them wanted to knock the other out. Splashes sounded off here and there but Mika couldn't afford to look. Audrey was good and Mika's shields were barely more than redirects.

She couldn't actually redirect because the whole point of the practice was to see how she could defend. And Mika could feel Malachi's sharp eyes on her.

He had to see it, but no one came to tap her on the shoulder.

And no one else noticed – too busy trying to keep from getting knocked into the icy water.

One last splash sounded off as the buzzer rang loud and clear.

Mika was sweating and shaking, exhausted but she also felt electric. She'd found a way around her disability and managed not to fuck it up.

"Twenty minute break to recharge, eat and drink some water. Then it's time for scrimmages!" Malachi yelled.

Audrey jogged over to her and Mika collapsed into a sitting position on the field. She had every intention of spending ten of those minutes doing absolutely nothing. All those pushups had made her arms feel like putty.

"Only a hundred people left," Audrey told her,

sitting down cross-legged beside her. "And we made halfway."

"Barely," Mika muttered, throwing herself onto her back so she could just...exist.

The sky was still clear and blue. There were no birds thanks to the freezing cold winter. The owls had stayed though, but they were all asleep at the moment.

Mika hadn't killed anyone so far.

It might be a good day after all.

"Hey, you two did excellent out there. And Mika! I knew you had some power, but that was insane!" Malachi plopped down next to them and Mika closed her eyes.

"Isn't this considered favoritism?" she asked, not wanting to sit up or look directly at Malachi. He'd taken off his shirt for the break and she refused to give him any indication she cared about the eight pack gloriously carved into his warm brown skin.

"Nah, I'm not giving you pointers or anything. I'll stop by a few other groups as well just to be safe," he teased. "Audrey, you're doing amazing. All that practice has really paid off."

"Doesn't hurt you trained me most of last semester," Audrey said with a laugh.

Mika hadn't known that, but it made sense.

"I told you I'd help you get on the team," Malachi said, quiet pride in his voice. "We need to remind everyone how strong human born witches are."

"Are you?" Mika asked, keeping her eyes shut.

"My mother was," Malachi murmured, as though the memory was painful.

She didn't ask why he used the past tense either.

"Drink some of the tonic water and make sure to eat," he warned them both. "The scrimmages are no joke and I want you both to make it. But as Mika pointed out, I can't play favorites."

The sound of him getting up made her crack open one eye and Mika admired his back and shoulders as he walked away. Gorgeous of course, with his black hair shaved close to his head. She wondered what he would look like with those tight curls grown out a little.

Malachi glanced back at them and smirked when he caught her looking.

Mika sat up and grumbled nonsense, annoyed with herself. "We should eat. This kind of magic uses up a lot of energy, but remember, not too much or you'll end up vomiting everywhere."

"Gross." Audrey wrinkled her nose. Then she pointed up toward the bleachers. "Wanna go eat with our fans?"

"Nope." She took Audrey's offered hand and let the other witch pull her to her feet. "We can't afford any distractions when we're this close."

They ate and went over their strategies again. Audrey would mainly defend and Mika would be offense. Together they would work on the circle strategy, always moving as they worked outward in wider circles until they'd invaded the other team's space and knocked them over the edge of the field into the water.

"This isn't going to be easy," Mika told her. "The three sections in enemy territory are there for a reason and we don't want to advance alone. We don't know the other players and have never practiced with them. It's going to be a clusterfuck and a half."

Audrey eyed the other players and nodded. "I'll lead as much as I can. I've got a loud voice and am good at bossing people around."

Instantly Mika was relieved. She didn't like talking, let alone yelling. "You're a leader," Mika agreed. "Come on, boss lady. Let's get this over with."

One hundred potential players. Malachi was already separating them into teams of ten instead of fifteen. Ten teams total. Five matches. At least scrimmages were only nine minutes long – three rounds of three minutes.

Mika glanced up at the faceless audience again.

It didn't matter that people were watching her, or that's what she tried to tell herself.

"Ready?" Audrey asked, pounding her fist against Mika's.

Mika smiled and gave Audrey a nod. "Ready as I'll ever be."

UNIVERSITY OF MORGANA

They were the last match. It was annoying, but Mika was also grateful. It gave them the most time to recover despite also being nerve-wracking as hell.

As the whole point of the game was to not get knocked into the water, and they needed eighty players to make up enough teams for the spring semester – getting knocked out wouldn't get anyone the tap.

They all had to wait until the end to see if their names made it onto the scoreboard.

So at least Mika didn't have to sit in a freezing wet uniform while healers did their thing, wondering for three more matches if she'd make it.

Finally, they were up and she cracked each finger to ease some of the tension in her body. Mika's magic was sitting up and taking notice. She felt ready and nervous all at the same time. They could only do their best, but now that she'd made it this far...

Mika felt like she had a stake in all this. She felt like

she actually cared, and that annoyed the hell out of her. She didn't *want* to care, but she also didn't want to be alone and isolated anymore.

They stepped onto the bridge from the underground hall that went around the field. The water sloshed underneath as players climbed out of it, shivering and cursing. Healers were waiting for them and Mika tried not to think of how cold that water was.

When her foot hit the field her whole body went on alert. She grabbed one of the practice masks and settled it over her face as Audrey did the same. The red bandana tied around her upper arm matched the others on their team. Their opponents were blue.

Three rounds of three minutes.

It would be fast and brutal and Mika lived for these short scrimmages.

Three minutes was long enough in her opinion – long enough to show the other team she wasn't fucking around. That she had the speed and strength to back up her attitude.

Mika tipped her head back and took a deep breath. It had been a long time since she'd been on a field and only now that she was here did she realize how much she'd truly missed it.

Audrey's shoulder brushed hers and Mika bent her knees and put her hands up like a fighter. Battle magic was a lot like boxing, or any hand-to-hand style of fighting. Her hunter training had always given her that extra edge.

The clock went up and whistles sounded off for everyone to prepare.

She and Audrey were positioned on the right side of the field, near the middle of their team. They'd all decided the diamond formation would be best since none of them knew each other well enough to do something more flashy and dangerous.

Someone hollered her and Audrey's name – generally being obnoxious as the cheers went up.

Then the bell rang and Mika tuned them all out.

Blue fired off immediately and three people on their team were instantly blasted into the water.

Audrey and Mika stepped forward as one, the other witch slightly in front of her to shield them both. Mika didn't conjure the energy ball she'd made earlier. Instead she summoned fire in one hand and earth in the other.

A clod of dirt hit an opponent in the face while another just barely shielded in time to block her fire. Audrey stepped forward, throwing an attack with one hand and shielding with the other. She stepped to the side to make room for Mika who was already summoning ice shards from the water below them.

Again they stepped forward as more players were knocked out. They kept circling each other, moving and moving. Heat blasted her side as Audrey jumped in front of her. Then a ball of energy came right at them – too big for either of them to shield against.

Mika stepped in front of Audrey and caught the ball. Audrey threw her hands up and shielded them both. They stepped forward, over the line and into the next square, their opponents throwing everything at them that they could.

But Audrey had cast an excellent shield.

"Now," Mika whispered.

The shield dropped and she sent that juiced up ball of energy at a group of three working together.

As the shield dropped something blasted her shoulder and she flew back. Mika scrambled for purchase on the field, but it was slick from the spells – one of the downsides to being last. She couldn't stop herself from sliding. She was going to go over.

"Gotcha!" Audrey declared triumphantly, diving after Mika.

Audrey had grabbed Mika's hand. Their skin was touching as she dangled over the edge.

Mika didn't dare look down. "Let me drop," she hissed, trying to make her fingers slide through Audrey's. The longer they were in contact the more danger Audrey was in. "Let. Me. Go."

"Figure it out, witchy bitch," Audrey snapped, throwing a shield over them just in time to avoid being roasted.

Her hands weren't tingling.

They had twenty seconds for Mika to get up or get out before the round ended.

Grunting she lifted herself up until she could put her feet against the edge of the field and then blasted power away from her. It sent her flying up and over until she landed in a heap on the field just as the first round ended.

"Don't ever do that again," she told Audrey, dusting

off her gear. "I'm trying out for you, but I refuse to be responsible for your death."

Audrey rolled her eyes. "You're so dramatic. Nothing even happened."

The second bell rang and they moved forward again, staying behind the remaining players on their team.

"You act like I'm making this all up," Mika snapped, throwing ball after ball of energy up and over the other players at their opponents so their teammates could advance forward. "Like I have control when I don't. Pushing my boundaries isn't going to help. It's just going to get someone killed."

She was pissed and tired and down to the dregs of her magic. Mika stomped down hard with the pure energy, making the field rattle with the force of her anger, unsettling their opponents. Audrey took advantage and knocked another out.

There were only three on the blue team left and four on theirs.

The bell clanged and Mika had to walk it off. She was practically foaming at the mouth.

Audrey had done nothing but help her since she'd arrived at Morgana and it was like the girl had a death wish. She kept testing Mika, pushing her. One of these times it wasn't going to end well, all because Audrey figured after nothing had happened a few times, it never would.

Mika ignored the glare Audrey was giving her and made sure she was behind everyone left.

The third and final bell clanged.

The blue team gave it their all, blasting everyone as hard and fast as they could.

Everyone went down, including Audrey. Everyone except Mika.

Fuck.

Mika didn't bother shielding as three opponents fired at her. She would never be able to hold one, and even a fire defense could only burn up so much magic before reaching her. Her best bet was to make herself an impossible target until Audrey could get up.

She dodged and ran, sliding under one attack, firing and then rolling to avoid another. Mika could feel the heat narrowly missing her back. Springing to her feet she ran over to Audrey who was holding a shield up against an onslaught of attacks.

Two splashes told her their other teammates were out.

One more minute and they would lose if they couldn't get their shit together.

Mika took the risk and threw up a wall of fire as she jumped in front of Audrey. It was just enough time for the other witch to get to her feet. Then a massive clump of dirt came through the wall of fire. It hit her right in the stomach, steaming and hot even through her gear.

The sound she made as it knocked all the air out of her was not feminine or graceful at all. Mika landed on her back and somehow managed to turn it into a backwards somersault so she was at least on her feet in a crouch.

But she couldn't breathe.

Gasping for air, she looked up to see Audrey shielding and firing all she had – standing in front of Mika just like they'd practiced.

Thirty more seconds.

Should she risk everything for a game?

Finally, she got air in her lungs. Mika stood and knew she had to make a split-second decision.

Audrey was the only one she'd touched skin to skin – multiple times, since she'd practically carried her the night before without the bone bracelet on – and had never once hurt her.

Mika couldn't shield for shit, but her power was raw.

She took one step forward and placed her bare hand on the back of Audrey's neck. Two words and power went down her arm and into the other witch.

Suddenly the shield flared and grew. They moved forward together, Mika's hand still on Audrey's neck. She didn't give her everything. She kept enough to build a ball of energy in her other hand similar to the one she'd used to blow apart the wooden dummy.

Over and over she said that word as they pushed the blue team back. The shield was strong enough Audrey was able to send it barreling into one of the other players, shoving him right over the edge of the field with a shriek into the water.

Thank Artemis Mika wasn't at full strength. If she had been, she never would have tried something this dangerous.

"Take it down when I say," Mika said, glancing at the clock. Fifteen seconds. "Blast the one on the right with everything you have, right at the ankles. I'll take the one on the left and aim him toward your dude."

Audrey nodded, no doubt unprepared for the invasion of Mika's magic – even if she did know what to do with it. Transferences weren't normally used because two witches had to have an affinity for each other.

But Audrey could do enchantments like no one Mika had ever seen before. She could turn an umbrella into an octopus and then back again – a spell so powerful it could blow up an entire building if done wrong.

Mika knew if she had an equal in strength and power – it would be Audrey. They'd been paired by the universe it seemed – and this was a risk worth taking.

Mika wanted to prove to Audrey she wasn't afraid. Well, she was, but...Audrey wanted this. It was worth the risk. And just because Mika was afraid, it didn't mean she couldn't still face that fear and do it anyway.

"Now," she whispered, eyeing the glittering ball of energy in her hand.

The shield dropped and Audrey did just as she'd asked.

Mika threw that energy ball toward the bigger of the two guys.

He flew backward into his teammate who was already unbalanced. The bell went off indicating the end of the round as both opponents hung over the edge like they were frozen in time.

Then they tumbled into the water just before the bell stopped.

Mika released Audrey and collapsed, falling to her knees hard, gasping for breath.

Audrey pulled off her mask and wiped the sweat from her brow, grinning and waving as the crowd went crazy.

They'd done it, and somehow...Mika hadn't killed anyone.

Everyone who had tried out and hadn't already been cut sat on the very bottom set of chairs that circled the field. They'd been reserved just for this.

Mika turned and found Kenzie and Selene waving at her while Ash and Finnick exchanged cash. She rolled her eyes and turned back to the field. She shouldn't have been surprised that they'd taken bets.

Malachi stood in the center of the field with a small smile on his face like he was proud of everyone for trying as hard as they did.

At least if she made the team, Mika felt like she could trust Malachi. For some reason she didn't think he would look down on her for not being able to shield.

"Thank you to everyone who gave their best today," Malachi said, projecting his voice so the acoustics made everyone able to hear him. "We have some really amazing contenders this year."

Audrey was jiggling her leg. Mika slapped her hand

over Audrey's knee and pressed down so she stopped. "You'll make it," Mika murmured. "Don't stress."

The other witch flung her arm over Mika's shoulders and grinned. "I knew you wouldn't hurt me."

Mika snorted, still not convinced that it couldn't happen one day. But for some reason her magic didn't attack Audrey – there had to be a reason why, something there for her to unpack and examine, but she filed it away for later.

There was a lot she needed to sort out later, but right now she could just be another college witch waiting to find out if she'd made the team.

The scoreboard started flashing names as Malachi talked.

"You've all been separated into your respective teams already," he said. "And you've all been grouped based on your individual skills and weaknesses so there shouldn't be any one team infinitely better than the others."

Mika wondered whose team Malachi would be on. Wouldn't that be unfair? Or would he put himself on the team with the least skilled players?

Then Audrey nearly choked Mika to death when she squeezed her tight. "Look! We're on the same team!" she practically screamed, pointing at the scoreboard.

But she was right, they were both on Team Black... and so was Malachi.

Mika couldn't help the smile that spread across her face, relief suffusing her entire body until she felt like she might just ooze off the chair into a puddle on the floor.

Cheers from the foxes, Kenzie, and Selene were

loudest of all, but Mika turned and saw Ethan and Lucien cheering as well. Ryan caught her eye and gave her a thumb's up, grinning like a madman.

More players jumped up and celebrated. Cheers filled the stadium as more names flashed onto the scoreboard and Mika hugged Audrey, hard. Audrey made a strangled noise, but she hugged Mika back with a laugh.

Too many emotions rattled around inside of Mika and she had no idea what to do with them. She was happy and scared and nervous, but more than anything she was grateful. Grateful for this witch who pushed her even when she snarled in retaliation – for the group of people who'd come to watch her try out...

Mika had people who cared about her here, and she could honestly say she'd never expected that to happen.

Coming to the University of Morgana had been the best decision she'd ever made.

"Congratulations to those who made the cut. To those who made it this far and didn't make a team, better luck next year. Don't stop training. You'll be the first tapped if anyone is injured." Then Malachi walked off the field and came right towards her and Audrey.

Audrey flung her arms around the massive witch and they both laughed as she nearly knocked him over. "You did great," Malachi said. "You earned this."

"Thanks to you and Mika," Audrey laughed, pulling back to shake Mika again.

Her joy was infectious and Mika grinned up at Malachi. "Looks like we'll be seeing you more often," she said, shrugging a shoulder.

Would he practice without a shirt on?

Mika cleared her throat and stood, offering him her hand. Surprisingly Hunter had brought her bone bracelet down to her after the match, and her magic was dampened once again.

Malachi shook her hand, not realizing how big this moment was for her – how easily she could kill him if she didn't bind her magic.

Apparently, only Audrey was immune.

"I'll be emailing everyone the information tonight, so don't get too hammered at the celebration." He walked off to congratulate the other players who'd made it before Mika could ask what he meant.

"Another party, woo!" Audrey screamed, running up the steps toward Kenzie and her foxes.

Mika was much slower, and her excitement was waning as she wondered if another party was really a good idea after what had happened the night before.

Ryan was gone when she looked for him. Mika figured she could bring him a muffin on Monday. When she looked up for Lucien and Ethan the hunter had disappeared too. He'd been there the last time. Mika wondered why he hadn't stuck around.

Then she reached the top where the foxes were and Ethan had made his way over. He waited for her with a smile, hands in his pockets. Mika stopped one stair below him, looking up at this impossibly tall, hot as fuck storm witch.

"I knew you liked dangerous things," Ethan told her.

For some reason that made her laugh. Mika went up

two steps and then turned, enjoying not having to crane her neck so much to look into Ethan's eyes. "You're not wrong," she admitted.

He tilted his head and studied her. No doubt she looked disgusting and sweaty and dirty.

"I'm uh, sorry. About what I said last night," Mika said, taking a step forward to wrap her arms around his neck.

Ethan took his hands out of his pockets and placed them on her hips. "Apology accepted."

"Just like that?"

"Yeah, just like that." Ethan grinned and then leaned down to kiss her. His lips tasted sweet like donuts and Mika sighed, melting into him. His strong arms wrapped around her waist and squeezed until her feet came off the stairs.

"Get it!" Finnick shouted.

Ethan laughed and released her. Mika's cheeks were red hot and she glared at the fox.

"Don't you have better things to do than be a creep?" Mika asked, taking a step away from Ethan.

"No," Finnick said with a shrug. "Plus Ethan is super pretty and I like eye candy."

Kenzie just laughed and rolled her eyes. "I'd say they're not always like this, but that would be a lie." The void witch came over and gave Mika a quick little hug. "Good job. I'm glad you were able to figure out a way to still join the team despite everything. We'll see you next Friday?"

It was weird being so close to Kenzie after a lifetime

of keeping their distance, but now they were more alike than Mika had ever thought possible. For someone who could strip her of her power permanently, Mika wasn't afraid. She wondered if this was how Audrey felt.

"Yeah," she agreed. "Next Friday."

Finnick and Ash hugged her even though she tried to push them off. They did the same to Audrey before leaving with Kenzie. Hunter and Selene lingered.

Mika glanced over at Ethan, but he was chatting with Audrey.

"I'll text you when I know when I'll be in San Francisco," Mika told Selene. "I was thinking tomorrow, but maybe next week since apparently I'm obligated to go celebrate."

Selene gave her that small smile and nodded. She stepped forward and gave Mika a quick hug. "I'll hold you to that. You were my only friend," she admitted. "My only *real* friend since no one else had the guts to come stay at our house."

They were both very careful not to look in Kenzie's direction.

"You deserved more from me," Selene murmured.

"And you deserved my honesty," Mika said. "We both fucked up. So...start fresh?"

Selene smiled for real this time. "Yeah, I'd like that." She kissed each of Mika's cheeks and it was second nature to return the gesture – their high society upbringing as bred into them as their power.

Then the matriarch of the Kavanagh clan trailed after her sister. Mika watched her go, hoping they would actually be able to become real friends again. She'd missed Selene and her quiet ways.

"I want you to read these books front to back by next Friday," Hunter told her, handing over a slip of paper. "And think about the question I wrote down. Next Friday we'll start working on your block."

Mika didn't know what to say to this alpha fox who terrified everyone but Kenzie. And apparently her. She looked up and studied Hunter's golden brown eyes, looking for the tells she could always see.

He was proud. Worried a little, but proud.

She didn't call him out on it. Mika just nodded and tucked the note into her pocket. "Will do, Teach. Can I ask you a question?"

Hunter glanced up at his mate and triad, but nodded.

"Why do you care about me? You hate everyone except those people up there." Mika watched for those tells, but he'd locked them down now.

"And Gram-Gram," Hunter said, but he didn't argue.

"Fine, five people." Mika rolled her eyes and crossed her arms over her chest. "Tell me and I'll be a model pupil."

Hunter grinned that terrifying smile that displayed his sharp canines, hands still in his pockets. Somehow it made him seem even scarier. He was a predator and so sure of his speed and strength he didn't need to worry about being unprepared for a chase.

He took a step forward and leaned in to whisper in her ear. "I'm drawn to chaos and pain. And you Mika, you have a lot of both."

His words chilled her blood.

Hunter took a step back and narrowed his eyes at her. "I see a lot of myself in you," he admitted. "And I don't wish that on anyone."

Mika didn't know what to say to that – didn't know how to feel. Hunter was known for his lack of empathy. He was a mercenary and a killer if the rumors were true. What did he see in her that was somehow familiar?

"It's not easy to be what they want you to be, when you know it will never be possible." Hunter looked up at Kenzie, patiently waiting for him. The way she looked at him—Mika had never seen love like that before. "But sometimes we get lucky, and we don't have to be anything but what we are."

Her hands were shaking and Mika had the distinct feeling this was one of those moments – a point in time she could look back on and say 'if I'd chosen differently...'

"I can teach you how to live with what you are, and help you find rules that will guide you through the difficult choices." Hunter studied her again and then nodded. "What you have is powerful and shaped by *you*, not the magic itself. So you have to decide who you are and what you want to be before that choice is taken from you."

The fox didn't bother saying goodbye. He just headed up the stairs, eyes only for Kenzie.

And Mika knew he was right. There was just one problem.

Who the hell was she?

"So, there's this party," Audrey told her as they walked through the forest toward Oleander House.

Mika was holding Ethan's hand. It was still a novel sensation. She couldn't stop staring at their hands, fingers laced together. No tingling from hers and no blood pouring from Ethan's pores.

The bone bracelet locked her shit down and Mika couldn't be more thankful to find this solution for her volatile power – even if it was temporary. She was under no illusions that this was a good way to live.

Three years she'd spent ignoring her magic, her block – everything that had happened that night. The only good thing that had come out of it was some small measure of control thanks to all her meditation and practice keeping it under lock and key.

Mika had locked down her emotions somewhere along the way as well. That had helped more than anything, but now...

Well, now she couldn't bottle everything up. She was at capacity and Mika had to figure out how to deal.

"I think we should go to the party," Audrey said, practically skipping along the path through the forest. Despite all the snow it felt a lot like spring. "We earned it after all."

Mika looked up at Ethan who was grinning down at her. "You did earn it," he told her. "And honestly I could do with a little drink right about now. That game is not easy to watch."

"Why didn't you try out?" Audrey asked, spinning around to walk backwards so she could see them both.

"I like working with plants." He smiled down at Mika. "Mika is enough excitement on her own."

Audrey snorted at that. "Ain't that the truth. Have fun with that."

"I intend to."

Mika was blushing and she almost pulled her hand out of his. It was all a little much to be honest. "Hey, can I talk to you?" She flashed Audrey an apologetic look. "Alone."

Her dorm mate held up her hands and grinned. "Hint taken. I'll see you back at the house. But you're not getting out of this party."

She nodded and watched Audrey walk down the path alone, humming as she made her way to Oleander House.

Then it was just her and Ethan.

For some reason she felt awkward and weird. Mika

pulled her hand out of his and wiped her sweaty palms on her pants. She had to make some things clear.

"Hey, don't worry. I'm not falling in love with you," Ethan teased.

Mika peered up at him. For some reason she didn't believe him, but at the same time the comment stung. She left it alone though, not ready for that conversation by any means.

"I actually wanted to ask what you and Lucien were doing together."

Ethan actually seemed flustered by her question and it made her even more curious. He leaned against one of the trees and shrugged, still smiling slightly. "He knocked on my door this morning and asked if I wanted to watch you try out for the team. Lucien brought coffee and donuts. That's hard to say no to."

So, she would have to ask Lucien for his motive then —why he'd sought Ethan out.

Crossing her arms over her chest she sighed. "You're sure this isn't weird? I mean, why go with him after last night?"

Ethan stopped smiling completely and looked up as the sky darkened. Clouds were rolling in – that or Ethan was conjuring them. "Lucien is hiding something. I don't trust him, and I want to know why he's so interested in you."

And there it was. Ethan was too perceptive for his own good. He had this way of reading people that never ceased to amaze her.

"I don't know why he's interested in me," Mika said

truthfully. "But we all have secrets. What makes you think his will hurt me? You're sure it's not because he kissed me?"

Ethan frowned then and the sky got darker. Mika shivered and wished she'd worn a heavier jacket.

"I told you I don't care about that," Ethan murmured. The wind picked up and Mika realized just how powerful of a storm witch he really was. "And I don't know if his secret will hurt you."

The temperature dropped even further but Ethan didn't seem to notice despite wearing just a long-sleeved shirt.

"But I can't know that if I don't know what it is." Ethan still hadn't moved from the tree, but snow started to fall, thick and fast.

This must be what it's like for others to deal with her magic.

Mika stepped forward and cradled Ethan's face in her hands, staring into those strange grey eyes that were dark and electric at the moment.

"His secret won't hurt me," Mika promised.

All of a sudden the wind died and the snow slowed, but the sun didn't come out again.

"You know what it is," Ethan said in surprise.

"I know his biggest secret," Mika agreed. She slid her hands back and into his thick curly hair. Ethan was tall and lean, but his muscles were rock hard. "Lucien won't hurt me. And even if he did, I can take care of myself."

He let out a deep breath and finally wrapped his arms around Mika. Ethan pressed his forehead against hers and closed his eyes. "I swear I'm not falling for you," he whispered.

Mika kissed him softly. "Liar," she murmured. "I nearly killed you and yet, here we are."

The laugh that escaped him was ragged and raw. "You underestimate my willingness to live, Mika, if it means I get one more kiss." Ethan's thumb traced her jaw and he opened his eyes to stare into hers.

When he kissed her Mika felt everything inside her rise up and nearly choke on the bracelet binding her magic. But she didn't care. Ethan tasted like rain. Her fingers gripped his hair hard and all she wanted was to be able to kiss him without the heavy silver between them.

Finally he pulled away and tapped her nose. "Don't worry; I know this is nothing serious."

Mika smiled at the joke. "Right, not serious at all. We're like...friends with benefits."

"Exactly," Ethan agreed. "Hugs count as benefits right? What about hand-holding?"

She nodded, smile widening. "And movie nights."

"Only if you like horror," he said very seriously.

The sun started peeking out through the dark clouds and Mika nodded. "We'll have to watch something tomorrow after coffee."

Ethan's grin dropped from his face when a scream pierced the air.

Mika's heart jumped into her throat. That sounded a lot like Audrey's scream.

They were frozen in place, staring at each other. Both

of them no doubt wondered if they'd actually heard it, or if the forest was playing tricks on them.

Then a second scream pierced the air.

Neither of them hesitated this time. They ran toward the sound as one, dodging trees and plowing through snow as quickly as they could. Ethan held out his hands and blasted a path with a gale-force wind.

The screaming didn't stop; it just got louder and louder as they tried to find its source among the trees.

Mika ran blindly, following her senses as her heart pounded. She ripped off her bone bracelet and suddenly the sound of blood pumping filled her ears until it drowned out even the sound of that endless screaming.

She clapped her hands over her ears and stumbled, but even that didn't quiet the noise. It took her too long to realize the sound wasn't her own blood, but someone else's.

Gasping, she ran toward it as the sound got louder and louder.

Ethan shouted, but she was too disoriented. Mika stumbled and fell, sprawling in the snow. Turning to see what she'd tripped over—the sound stopped.

Not even an owl called out. Wind didn't rustle through the trees. There was absolute silence as she stared at a body brutally staked to a tree.

Blood was everywhere. It soaked the tree and the snow. It covered Mika and she could feel it singing to her – a crystal clear note as she held up her hand to see the blood covering it just like that night three years ago.

She forced herself to look at the body pinned to the tree like a dead butterfly behind glass.

It wasn't Audrey.

Mika sucked in a massive breath of air and scrambled back.

She didn't recognize the witch, but she was sliced open from neck to navel.

"Fucking hell," Ethan muttered. "They stripped her organs."

He was right. Her chest and abdomen were nothing but a cavity.

The blood sang as it soaked into the snow.

This girl had been murdered in cold blood —*sacrificed*.

The silence in the forest was deafening.

Don't miss Wicked Games
Book 2 in this slow burn witch academy series

Need something to pass the time? Have you read Kenzie and her foxes series yet? It's a completed trilogy!
For Fox Sake
All Foxed Up
What the Fox

OTHER BOOKS BY EMMA DEAN

REVERSE HAREM SHIFTER/PARANORMAL
ROMANCE*

Chaos of Foxes Series

For Fox Sake

All Foxed Up

What the Fox

University of Morgana Academy Series

Something Wicked

Wicked Games

Standalones

Spotted Her First

Seeing Spots

A Bandit's Prequel

Make Out Like Bandits

Vaudeville Runaway

BLUE MOUNTAIN WOLF PACK (M/F WOLF SHIFTERS)

Alpha Wolf

Broken Wolf

THE DRAGA COURT SERIES (POLYAM/RH LIKE GAME OF THRONES IN SPACE WITHOUT THE INCEST)

Princess of Draga

Crown of Draga

Jasmine of Draga

Heir of Draga

Queen of Draga

Fate of Draga

Prequel Novella – Royal Guard of Draga*

Christmas Epilogue Novella - Winter Solstice in Draga

*Can be read as a standalone before or after Princess of Draga, but in the timeline takes place before Princess.

*All paranormal stories are in the same universe - the Council of Paranormals.

Want updates on when the books are released and my

progress with them?

Sign up for my newsletter @ emmadeanromance.com

WANT FREE STORIES?

If you subscribe to my newsletter you can get these shorts free!

A Bandit's Prequel

(Short steamy reverse harem shifter story.)

Royal Guard of Draga

(Novella prequel for a Game of Thrones in space slow burn story that turns into a reverse harem, this is also steamy and just the beginning.)

ABOUT THE AUTHOR

Emma Dean lives and works in California with her husband and son. She loves romance but needed something different so Draga Court was born. Council of Paranormals was soon to follow when her shifters came to life.

With too many stories to write the schedule has been filled through 2019.

When she's not writing she's reading, or spending time with her family.

At least now that she's publishing she has an excuse for not folding the laundry ;-)

Follow her on Social Media or
www.emmadeanromance.com

facebook.com/emmadeanromance

bookbub.com/authors/emma-dean

ABOUT THE AUTHOR

Emma Dean lives and works in California with her husband and son. She loves romance but needed something different so Draga Court was born. Council of Paranormals was soon to follow when her shifters came to life.

With too many stories to write the schedule has been filled through 2019.

When she's not writing she's reading, or spending time with her family.

At least now that she's publishing she has an excuse for not folding the laundry ;-)

Follow her on Social Media or
www.emmadeanromance.com

f facebook.com/emmadeanromance

BB bookbub.com/authors/emma-dean

52530307R00173

Made in the USA
San Bernardino, CA
07 September 2019